Summer's Glory

MARY JANE HATHAWAY

DEDICATION

This book is dedicated to anyone who has ever had to reach for grace, and all who have waited on forgiveness from those they had hurt.

"Though your sins are like scarlet, they shall be as white as snow; though they are red as crimson, they shall be as wool." Isaiah 1:18

CONTENTS

CHAPTER ONE

"Adopt the pace of nature: her secret is patience."
— Ralph Waldo Emerson

"Thor, stay."

Violet Tam wasn't worried about leaving her mastiff unattended. He always followed her commands and could certainly handle any strangers who might think a dognapping was a good idea. But the summer heat was hard on a dog his size and they needed to hurry. The enormous, fawn-colored animal sat with a dignified, but faintly unhappy air. Violet shifted the blue bin to her hip and pulled open the door to the elementary school. Holding it open with her foot, she waited for her friend Jamie Lawson to squeeze by with a cardboard box.

"This is the beginning of summer. For real. I don't care if the official date is next week. It's summer already." Jamie huffed her unhappiness as she walked toward the eighth grade classroom and slid the box onto the long wooden table in the front. It was hotter in the classroom than it was outside but the air conditioning wouldn't be turned on until the kids came back.

"Before we became friends, I thought teachers got the summer off," Jamie said, wiping sweat from her forehead. "I don't know why I put on make-up today. I should have just rolled out of bed and come straight down here."

"You'd still be beautiful," Violet said, smiling at the idea of Jamie spending the day rearranging the classroom in her nightgown and slippers. "And thank you for helping me."

"My pleasure. I mean, not really. Just a saying, of course, but you know what I mean."

"I do," Violet said.

Jamie peered into the box. "More books?"

"Always the tone of surprise," Violet said.

"It's just that—" she picked one out of the box "—does anybody read Agatha Christie anymore? In fact, does anybody read? It's like there are just a few people reading all the books, and everybody else reads one or two a year. What are the chances one of your students is going to want to read through all of these? Aren't all the kids watching The Walking Dead or playing video games?"

Violet frowned. "It's not a matter of finding that one ravenous read. It's basic cultural literacy. Like knowing what Star Wars is. Everybody should read at least one Christie novel." She looked into the box. "Oh, and Arthur Conan Doyle, Dorothy L. Sayers, Mickey Spillane—"

"Okay, I get it." Jamie started to laugh. "I'm sorry I asked. The more time I spend around you, the longer my reading list is. I'm never going to finish it before I die. If you don't make me carry them all over the county and I'll be happy."

"We only have one more trunk load of boxes. Eyes on the prize, remember?"

"You mean the oven-fired pizza waiting for us at the end of this?"

"Exactly. I'm ordering the feta, spinach and sun dried tomato." Violet hadn't been keen on her mother's plan to start a restaurant with wood-fired ovens. In fact, she'd thought it was downright weird. Then she'd tasted the fantastic garden-fresh, locally sourced dishes and decided it had been a stroke of genius after all. Fire and Brimstone had been popular from the day it opened. People in Arcadia Valley couldn't get enough of the place.

"I can't wait." Jamie paused, draping herself over the box. "You know, I never knew people like your mom could run a pizza joint."

"What do you mean?" Violet tried not to jump to conclusions but anger flared in her at the phrase 'like your mom'. Jamie hadn't seemed racist in the months since they'd become good friends but it wouldn't be surprising if she thought Asian people should all run Chinese food restaurants.

"You know. She's so earthy. Like you, making your own goat cheese and lavender soap."

"I still don't see the conflict," Violet said. "A natural lifestyle means enjoying the world more, not less. And it's not exactly a pizza joint. There are a few other dishes like baked potatoes and pot pie."

"But everybody orders the pizza," Jamie pointed out. "Maybe they like watching it cook and then seeing it pulled out of the oven on those big wooden paddles—"

"It's called a peel."

"Right, that. Anyway, she's always been about the farmers market and the goats and the..." She waved her hands. "Herbs and stuff."

Violet rolled her eyes. "Pizza has herbs. Growing our own food doesn't mean we don't interact with the community. I think it's the opposite, really, especially when we had a booth at the farmers market. We saw everybody. You grew up on a blueberry farm. Don't you think it brought you closer to everyone in Arcadia Valley?"

"Not really. We saw people during the season, I guess. And the booth at the market was the same way. Lots of people in the summer but for the rest of the year, the grocery store is where you meet everybody," Jamie said. She straightened up, eyes wide. "I forgot to tell you that I met the cutest guy in the dairy aisle yesterday. He said his name is Silas Black. You know him?"

Violet hesitated one second too long. "Sure, I know him." She could see it so clearly. When Silas walked into a room, everybody took notice. He was tall, dark and handsome, but it was a certain something, a brooding quality combined with a crackling intensity that made Silas unforgettable. She could imagine how Jamie felt when she first saw him. Silas probably laid on the charm and Jamie was swept off her feet, the way girls always were. Unless you were the kind of girl Silas didn't think deserved any charm. Then you tried your hardest to stay out of his way.

"Uh oh. I saw that." Jamie narrowed her eyes. "And don't pretend you didn't just hesitate there."

Violet ignored her friend. "We should hurry. Thor's waiting outside in the heat. Plus, if we don't get those last boxes in here, we're going to hit the dinner rush. I don't want to wait thirty minutes for my pizza."

Jamie looked like she was going to argue, but instead said, "Your mom wouldn't bump your order up to the front of the line?"

"Never! She's a professional." Violet headed for the car, glad that Jamie hadn't decided to pry any more information from her.

She paused to give Thor an extra scratch on her way past. He lifted his head and fixed her with a look, as if he could tell she was upset. Thor would be the only one who noticed because Violet was determined to keep the past in the past, and her drama to herself. She'd self-medicate with ice cream and cry into Thor's coat later, but for now, she wasn't going to give any hint that Silas Black had any control over her life.

As they lifted the last two boxes from the trunk and carried them inside, Violet forced herself to keep her smile in place. Now that she'd had a few minutes to accept Jamie's words, it wasn't such a big deal. It was bound to happen. She'd already run into Silas once, very briefly. It was a small town and she couldn't expect to avoid him completely, as wonderful as that would be.

The Lord is my strength and my shield. Violet repeated the psalm to herself as they set the last boxes in the classroom. The old grade school rhyme about sticks and stones hadn't been true, but she was stronger now. She wasn't a little girl anymore. She could handle whatever Silas Black threw her way, and this time she wouldn't suffer in silence.

Silas tapped the front of the menu. "Summer's Glory?"

Looking up, Luke Delis nodded. "The ingredients are seasonal. They swap out the menus depending on what time of year it is. The summer is the best in my opinion but Nico thinks winter is better, probably because they use a lot more of his products."

Silas hoped they still had Nico Delis's artisanal meats on the menu. Luke pulled the winning lotto ticket with his large Greek family, but being brothers with the town's butcher had to be the best perk. Stavros and Theo, Luke's other brothers, were clearly made from the same Delis mold but if Silas had to choose, he'd rather be related to an artisan butcher than a teacher, a therapist, or a pediatrician. Of course he'd never tell Luke that. Or maybe he would because Luke and his love for steaks would probably agree with him.

Silas scanned the menu, surprised by the variety. Even the drink list was a whole page long. Homemade sodas using natural sweeteners, organic mint teas and lemonade flavored with fruit, and free trade coffee. He'd had his heart set on French fries but he'd forgotten they didn't offer any fried food.

If it couldn't be cooked in the wall-length stone ovens at the back of the restaurant or mixed up fresh, they didn't have it.

Luke waved at a group being seated across the large space and Silas noted the full tables. Rural Idaho wasn't known for its culinary novelties and Mrs. Tam had tapped into the need for something other than fast food. Sure, there were twenty ways to prepare the state's biggest crop, the potato, but most of them went to processing plants to make potato chips. Fire and Brimstone was truly a unique twist on the local food scene.

The wide open space had been converted from an old automotive garage and one side still sported sliding doors. The brick walls had been scrubbed of paint and the hanging lights were naked Edison bulbs protected by antique blue mason jars. With the metal chairs and the vintage gas station signs on the walls, Silas wouldn't know whether he was in a garage or a restaurant if he didn't see mouth-watering food being brought to the tables all around him.

"So, how's the book?" Luke nodded at the paper back Silas had brought with him to read. Luke was perpetually late. Maybe it was because Luke was a doctor who might be called to an emergency, or maybe it was a personality trait, but Silas made sure to have something to read while he waited for his friend.

"Good. I've read it before." At least six times before,

but he didn't say that part. It was perfectly acceptable to read mysteries. It was even okay to read classic mysteries from the fifties. But people might think he was weirder than they already did if he admitted to reading the same books over and over.

"I can't decide. I think I'll order one with the kimchi and one with the barbeque pork and red chili sauce." Luke Delis frowned at the little paper card.

"Two? I thought doctors were supposed to be health nuts. Wouldn't it make more sense to get half and half?"

"Of course it would. But what about leftovers? Won't Loki want a piece?"

"Mastiffs need more than a piece of pizza, Luke."

"Well, get her a whole pizza. As for me, I'm a growing man and I need sustenance."

"Pretty sure you're done growing, unless you mean sideways."

Luke grinned. "That's disappointing to hear. I guess I'll always be shorter than you."

"Everybody's shorter than me. Even your brothers." At six foot five, he was used to looming over everyone, even the four Delis brothers. Stavros, Nico, Luke and Theo had all inherited their mother's looks, their father's height, and a mischievous sense of humor. If they weren't such nice guys, they could cause some real havoc in town. As it was, they had always been the kind of kids everyone was glad to see. Not like

Silas. Nobody had wanted him around and he'd liked it that way.

"How are the orders coming along? We haven't had a master carpenter in Arcadia Valley for a long time. I think the closest is in Twin Falls and he's booked up for months. Probably everybody is knocking on your door." Luke asked.

"The Bodkins' new pantry is almost ready. I'll probably install it tomorrow. I made some gun cabinets to for Ron Taylor and I'll deliver those in the day or so. And then I've got a big project happening. Right here, actually."

"Really?" Luke looked around. "What's the plan?"

"Mrs. Tam wants a long bar that wraps around that side of the restaurant. More seating for the lunch crowd that just pops in for a slice or a salad." He pointed to the wall across from the ovens. "Then another built-in counter near the door for people who are waiting for tables. They can have a drink and watch the food cooking without crowding the entrance. Mrs. Tam says it will keep the restaurant moving smoothly and people out of the way of the servers."

Luke looked like he was trying not to laugh.

"What?" Silas asked.

"It's just… you called her Mrs. Tam. Like you're still fourteen"

"I just can't call her Shirley. She'll always be Mrs. Tam to me." Silas didn't feel like he had permission to call her by her first name. Not because Mrs. Tam herself minded. It was simply the past inserting itself again.

"Anyway, the counter sounds great."

"I hope it will be. It'll take a lot of time to measure and install, especially since some of the work has to be done on site after closing or early in the morning."

"Sounds like you're getting a lot of work coming your way," Luke said.

"I'm definitely busy. Your brother came by and asked me about reworking some of his kitchen."

"Which brother?"

"The one with the old house and the new girlfriend," Silas said. "You think you'll be best man?"

His brows went up. "Nico? It's true they're already talking about getting married, but they just met, really. I thought they'd have a long engagement. At least a year." He paused. "Ok, I guess they've been going out a few months but really, in the scheme of things, they just met."

"He didn't say anything to me. I just got the impression it was pretty serious since he'd asked her opinion on the kitchen remodel. You don't like her?" Things would get complicated if the rest of the family didn't like Nico's girlfriend. Silas had only seen her at Arcadia Valley's library, where she was the director, but he'd gotten the impression she would fit right in with the Delis family. He was good at getting a feel for a person. That's what had made him such a good con artist. Those days were behind him, but the skill of reading someone hadn't gone away.

"No, I think she's great. I'm just surprised." Luke seemed to be having trouble absorbing the idea of his older brother getting married again. "They do spend a lot of time together. They have this thing about working in the garden. I mean, I love my garden. Nothing like fresh tomatoes, but they're really into it. She keeps talking about what she's going to grow next. She might be a little obsessed."

Silas smiled and said nothing. Luke would think he was crazy if he learned how much time Silas spent in his garden. It was one of the biggest draws to returning to Arcadia Valley. He knew the seasons and what kind of produce grew well. He wasn't a picky eater, but he could never get used to store bought vegetables. They seemed almost flavorless.

Luke went on. "After Laura died, he just never seemed interested in anybody. Seems kind of sudden."

Silas shrugged. "Not that I know much about it, but I think that's the way it happens. You never hear about people falling for each other after being friends for ten years."

"Or enemies," Luke said. "I think that's just something girls picked up from Pride and Prejudice where the guy acts likes a jerk and the girl falls for him anyway."

Silas laughed. "They all want Mr. Darcy but if we acted

like that in real life, we'd never get another date." He'd done much worse than Mr. Darcy and although a lot of people in town were willing to give him another chance, there were some who would never come within a mile of him again, and he didn't blame them. God had forgiven him, but plenty of people weren't going to follow His lead.

"Hey, guys." A voice sounded over Silas's shoulder and he turned to see Stavros, Luke's brother. "Silas," he said, offering his hand. "Good to see you."

Silas shook his hand, wishing he felt comfortable thanking Stavros for what he did on a daily basis. A therapist for juvenile delinquents the bookish younger brother had a quiet way about him that Silas had seen before. It was the calm and surety of a man who knew his purpose in life. There had been a man like that where Silas had been incarcerated, a person who took the time to reach out to every young man who might be looking for help. "I thought you lived in Pocatello." *Where I used to be locked up*, he didn't add.

"He does. Just back for a quick meeting," Luke explained. "He already harassed me this morning. Now it's round two, I guess."

Stavros grinned. "Always a pleasure. And maybe you're following me. This is my favorite place to eat." He held up his cardboard box of leftovers. "Fire and Brimstone is vegan friendly."

Silas tried to cover his surprise. How strange that Stavros was a vegan and Nico was a butcher. Luke caught his eye and smiled, knowing exactly what he was thinking. "We're all about diversity and freedom, as long as you think Greeks are the best," Luke said with a deadpan expression.

"Ahh, well, my Irish ancestors might disagree but since my family is more recently hailing from Louisiana, I think I'll just keep my mouth shut." Silas mimed zipping his lips.

"Louisiana, really?" Stavros sounded surprised.

"Sure. I still have cousins there. My mom always said she was going back to visit someday but…" His words trailed off into an awkward silence.

"I'm sorry to hear about your mom," Stavros said.

"Thank you." Silas cleared his throat.

"We have more mom than we need. We can loan you some extra whenever you need any," Luke said.

Stavros choked out a laugh. "I'm telling her you said that."

"Go ahead, pipsqueak." Luke lifted a fist and narrowed his eyes.

Still laughing, Stavros said, "Well, I've gotta go. See you guys later." He waved good bye and was gone.

"Small town. You don't just see all your friends but you're related to half of them." Luke's expression changed to one of surprise. "Hey, that's Violet and Jamie by the door." He stood up and waved.

Silas glanced toward the door and felt his heart sink to his shoes. Jamie was grinning and waving back. Violet looked just the same as she had a few weeks ago. Maybe a little more flushed from the heat. Her silky black hair was cut in a sharp bob just below her chin and she was dressed casually in a T-shirt and jeans. Silas was suddenly aware of the fact he hadn't changed from working all day in the shop and he brushed at the light film of sawdust still clinging to the sleeves of his plaid shirt.

He said quickly under his breath, "I'm sure they want to eat alone. Let's say 'hi' and let them sit somewhere else."

Luke only had time to throw him a confused look before Violet and Jamie arrived at their table.

"It's like a class reunion," Luke said and Silas wanted to drop through the floor.

"Yeah, the joys of living in a small town. You get to see your high school classmates every day." There was an edge to Violet's voice.

"Why don't you guys sit with us?" Luke pulled out a chair on either side of the table.

"Are you sure? We don't want to interrupt your guy time." Jamie was already settling into the chair beside him.

Violet stood there, unmoving. She had fixed her eyes on Jamie as if hoping the woman would hear her unspoken plea and get up.

Silas cleared his throat. "We'd love for you to join us."

It seemed as if she wasn't going to respond but after several seconds, Violet slowly lowered herself into the chair next to him.

"Hey, look." Jamie reached out and grabbed the paperback. "Looks like something Violet would read."

Silas seriously doubted that. Maybe the cover reminded Jamie of a Gothic romance. "More people have seen the movie."

Violet leveled a look at him. "You always have a smooth explanation ready."

He blinked in surprise. She was quoting from the Maltese Falcon, Joel Cairo to be exact. He'd read that line not five minutes before. "What do you want me to do? Learn to stutter?" he quoted back.

She didn't smile at their exchange. He felt his stomach drop at the uncomfortable parallels between himself and Sam Spade. Sly, shifty, and always making sure he came out on top.

Luke looked from Violet to Silas, and seemed to decide he didn't want to know what they were saying. "So, what have you guys been up to today?" he asked Jamie.

"We've been moving boxes into my classroom all day. We're not really fit for company," she said.

"What? You both look great," Luke said, giving them

each an appreciative smile. "Hey, Violet, did you know Silas has a mastiff, too?"

She looked at him for the first time. Her expression wasn't one of pleasant surprise. "I did not."

Luke went on. "That's pretty weird, isn't it? How many people have that kind of dog? I don't even think I'd seen one before Thor, and now there are two." Silas tried to give Luke a 'change the subject' look, but he didn't seem to notice. He went on, "You know how people look like their pets? Well, Loki is really tall and all black."

"Oh, but that thing about people resembling their dogs wouldn't work for Violet," Jamie said, holding up a finger. "I mean, Thor is huge and some of Violet's eighth graders are taller than she is."

Silas didn't want to comment but found himself saying, "Thor, as in Chris Hemsworth?"

"As in son of Odin. You know, Norse mythology," she answered. Her tone implied that he, in fact, did not know. "So, you named your dog Loki. As in Tom Hiddleston?" Violet asked. Her expression said that she already knew the answer.

"As in Loki, enemy of Thor. You know, Norse mythology," Silas said.

Jamie stared, looking from Silas to Violet. "That's weird. Isn't that weird? I mean, how many people have that kind of dog and then name them after somebody related to smiling as she laughed. He had never heard her laugh before and it was a beautiful sound, just like her. "But seriously, I wasn't the one who got the bloody nose and landed on the hard floor."

She winced. "I think hitting the floor hurt more than running into that tube."

"Really?" Alarm shot through him. "Did you hit your head? I didn't see very clearly. I was too busy trying to figure out what I'd run into. Do you need to get checked out? Let me feel for a bump." He reached out, ready to examine the back of her head. Thor let out a low growl and Silas paused his movement in mid-air. "They say a slight concussion can— "

"No, not my head. It's... the other end." Her cheeks went pink.

"Oh." He dropped his hands. "Not much you can do for that."

"Right. Not like they can put a cast on it."

He snorted. "That would be awkward."

"Teaching middle schoolers in a butt cast? Recipe for epic teasing. I'd never live it down." She was laughing but her smile started to waver as the words hung between them.

An awkward silence followed. Silas searched for something to say. "How did the tomato harvest go yesterday?"

"They picked everything that was ripe and are blanching it all today. She's got some friends helping," Violet said. "How's the farm going?"

"My mom planted the usual crops, but got too sick to really spend much time with it. My sister Romy took over."

"Well, if she ever needs help, let us know."

His brows went up. Surely she didn't mean that.

"I know how important the farm was to your mom. She brought a lot of produce to the school for kids to bring home if they wanted," Violet said.

"I didn't know she did that."

She nodded. "Hunger is an issue in every town and she wanted reach beyond the foodbanks. A lot of kids would take apples, carrots, cucumbers or whatever they wanted. It was a good way to get healthy food to kids who might not have enough at home. You never knew who really needed it, so there was no shame attached."

"Sounds like her," he said, his voice rough. "Romy is worried about disappointing our mom. I thought she meant keeping the garden alive but I can see that it's more than that."

He struggled to swallow back his grief. It hadn't been long enough since his mother had died for him to be able to talk about her without feeling overwhelming sadness. The cancer had progressed quickly and he was thankful they'd all had a chance to say goodbye, but it didn't keep him from missing her so much it took his breath away. She'd always believed he would find his way home and back to his faith. At least she'd lived long enough to see it.

Looking at Violet standing there, still holding the daisies, he suddenly wished he had asked his mother's advice before she died. Maybe she would have known how to repair the damage he'd done, known the words to somehow bring peace to his past.

Violet held his gaze and something in those beautiful dark eyes gave him hope. Maybe all was not lost. She hadn't refused to let him in the restaurant. She'd accepted the flowers a lot more easily than he'd expected. Thor hadn't bitten his hand off. Maybe all he needed was the courage to say what was in his heart. He took a breath, trying to calm his racing pulse. He'd had to apologize to a lot of people in the last few years and one more shouldn't make a difference, but it did. She was different.

Then, as he fought for the strength to speak honestly, she seemed to sense he was on the verge of saying something important, and turned away.

"I'll go put these in a vase," she said, and seconds later had disappeared into the kitchen.

Silas was left standing there, heart pounding, unspoken words on his tongue. Thor followed after her, but stopped for a moment to give Silas a long look.

"Don't worry. Not going to chase after her," Silas said under his breath. Fine, he had work to do anyway. If God wanted them to make up, then He would have to keep Violet in the same room with him for more than five minutes. Silas had done his best and he wasn't going to force her to listen to him, no matter how much he wanted her to.

CHAPTER SEVEN

"The mountains are calling and I must go."

— John Muir

Violet placed the daisies in the clear blue vase and plucked off dead leaves. The Sayers book was incredible. She'd never seen a copy that old. She glanced at it again, smiling. Books always made good presents, but a vintage book by a favorite author was a great present.

She'd never been a person who needed gifts to feel valued. She'd rather have someone's attention and time. But he'd brought her flowers. And not just any flower. He'd brought her daisies, her favorite. Of course, it was just a coincidence. He couldn't have known it was her favorite flower. No one had ever brought her flowers. She'd dated a few guys in college and even gone out with Tom Bedford, Arcadia Valley's handsome young electrician, a few times. But none of them had thought to give her any flowers, not even roses, which she'd always thought were horribly cliché.

Violet straightened the flowers, admiring the bright white of the petals, the golden centers, and the impossibly green leaves. It really didn't matter. She was modern, smart, and professional. That old idea of wooing a woman with a bunch of dead vegetation had no effect on her. None at all. But she couldn't help smiling. She felt warmth in the center of her chest, as if something wonderful had happened. She always felt better around plants. The garden was one of her favorite places to spend time.

Daisies were such a friendly flower. It would have been strange if he'd brought her red roses. Or even yellow roses, for friendship. They weren't friends. Nothing close to it. Orchids would have been strangely formal. A potted plant would have looked more like a housewarming gift. But daisies were perfect, somehow. They were cheerful and unassuming. A simple peace offering. But her happiness came from the unexpected beauty, not because they were from Silas. Violet repeated the words to herself but the smile didn't fade from her lips.

She wondered whether to put them at the front for all

the guests to enjoy, or to have them in the office. She decided to leave them on the desk while she worked on her lesson plans, and then bring them out when the lunch crowd arrived. Of course, if Jamie or her mother saw the flowers, they might ask where they'd come from and get the completely wrong idea.

At the thought of her mother, Violet remembered what she'd forgotten yesterday. Carrying the daisies to the office, she told Thor to stay and headed for the main part of the restaurant. The sound of hammering echoed through the cavernous space. She stopped a few feet away from where Silas knelt near the window and cleared her throat. He didn't look up.

"Excuse me, Silas," she said loudly, feeling formal and awkward.

He turned, startled. "Yes?"

"I forgot to ask you something. My mother wanted to know if you could also make some butcher block cutting stations in the kitchen. She said you might want to look at the space before deciding."

"Now?"

"Whenever is easiest. I can wait." She should have stayed in the office for a while and let him get some work done. He probably felt like he'd never finish the project with all the time he spent talking to her.

"I can take a look right now, if you're okay with that." He stood up and Violet realized he was trying to be considerate of her, in case she felt uncomfortable being alone with him in an isolated part of the building. She almost laughed at the thought.

It didn't make any difference whether they were out in the main restaurant section with the full wall of glass windows or back in the kitchen. Violet wasn't afraid of Silas, not in that way. She was wary of him, true. But the only physical danger apparently came from her inability to slow down around dark corners.

She led him through the swinging double doors, hitting the bank of lights on the right. The kitchen sprang into view. Violet couldn't help smiling with pride. Every surface gleamed, the floor shone, copper pots hung above the counters, long rows of large knives hung on magnetized metal strips, and the shelves were stocked with neatly labeled tubs. Her mother had worked for forty years as a paralegal and saved all her life for this chance. She wasn't going to cut corners.

Silas let out a low whistle. "Very nice."

"Makes you want to cook, doesn't it?" Violet pointed at the end of the room. "She was thinking of putting in the butcher blocks down here, near the walk-in freezers. They're using portable work stations right now, but wheeling them in and out of the storage area is a hassle."

He followed her across the room and when they reached the freezers, she stood back so he could examine the space. It was strange to see him so focused as he measured and took notes. An odd sensation passed over her, of seeing something from the past and something completely new, like an overlay from the projector she used at school. He was the boy who had made her life a misery, but the harder she looked at him, the less resemblance he bore to the monster she knew.

She watched him work, her mind and her heart at odds. Grown up Silas was careful, competent, and kind. He made toys for children and sat with old ladies in church. He brought daisies to girls who didn't even like him. But the boy Silas had always been charming like that. He'd used his good looks and that easy grace to convince people he was the good guy. A little dangerous, but all in good fun. Violet had been the only one who could see through his lies. Maybe he hadn't really changed. Maybe Violet's talent to see through him had faded away. What if she was now as gullible as the rest of the world?

Silas looked up at that moment and their gaze met. His expression was guarded, his eyes held a question. He waited for her to speak. When she said nothing, he didn't move. She was aware of the moment stretching between them and she knew that she should say something, anything. It was her chance to confront him about everything he had done.

She didn't want an apology. She wanted *an explanation.*

Violet clenched her fists and tried to organize her thoughts. Silas straightened up and stood before her, hands at his sides, clearly waiting for her to give voice to her anger. He seemed sad, but resigned.

Seconds passed.

She opened her mouth but didn't know where to start. Maybe with the fortune cookies he used throw at her in the hallway. Maybe with the way he laughed when she changed direction to avoid him. A memory flashed in her head of the months he sat behind her in eight grade history class, kicking the back of her chair and whispering fake Chinese words under his breath.

"I'm Korean, not Chinese," she blurted.

"I know."

He swallowed hard and that small movement broke her resolve. She had waited years to confront him and now she felt pity for the man before her.

Anger and frustration flooded through her. Silas had just lost his mother to cancer and was doing the best he could to live an honorable life. She had so much to say to him, so many questions she needed answered. And now she couldn't speak the words to the man standing before her, his head slightly bent as if in preparation for her tirade.

Turning on her heel, Violet strode out of the kitchen, back down the hallway, and into the office. Slamming the door behind her, she threw herself into the office chair, then bolted upright, crying out in pain. Clenching her teeth against the throbbing in her backside, she started to cry. Thor pushed his head into her lap and stared up at her with large brown eyes.

"I'm fine," she said to Thor, then sobbed harder at how big a lie it was. Silas was making her miserable now, just as he always had been. He may not have said or done anything to her, but it was clear there was too much bad history for her to be anything close to professional. A bunch of daisies couldn't fix their problems. Her heart felt bruised and her nerves were ragged.

Violet cried hot tears into Thor's coat. Her nose was running and she absent-mindedly reached for Silas's handkerchief, which she had cleaned and left neatly folded on the desk. She wiped her tears and blew her nose, then realized what she was holding. Tossing it onto the desk, she reached for some tissues instead. The Dorothy L. Sayers book seemed to smirk at her, mocking her for putting so much importance on something so silly.

All of her talk about being cold and detached was just that— talk. She would never be indifferent to Silas Black. He would always have control over her emotions. Nothing she could do would protect her from that. Her only defense was to avoid him completely.

Silas forced himself to finish measuring the end of the work space. His palms were sweaty and his heart was pounding in his chest. As Violet faced him, that expression of fear and anger on her face, he had remembered all of the times he had bullied her. Giving Violet a bloody nose hadn't been as shocking as that expression on her face. Acid rose in his throat and he closed his eyes for a moment. He was forgiven, made new, complete in Him.

It didn't mean he wouldn't suffer the consequences of his actions, but God had forgiven him, even if Violet had not.

He wrote down the final numbers and winced at the shakiness of the notes. Since arriving in Arcadia Falls, he'd thought about her often but he hadn't really been aware of how desperately he'd wanted her forgiveness. For the first time, he had to face the fact that he had been holding onto that hope. More than hope. He'd imagined they could put it all behind them, maybe even be friends. He could convince her he was different now, not the jerk she'd known in school, and they'd find peace. But nothing he could do would make a difference.

Replacing the measuring tape on his tool belt, Silas tried to refocus on the task at hand. He had a job to do. As a master carpenter, he held his craft to the highest standard. He couldn't let what was happening between Violet and himself have any bearing on his work. As hard as it would be, Silas needed to push every thought of her from his head and his heart. If God wanted them to be reconciled, it would happen. Otherwise, as much as he hated the thought, he'd just have to live with the unresolved pain between them.

CHAPTER EIGHT

"Calligraphy of geese

against the sky-

the moon seals it."

— Yosa Buson

"How's the new job?" Luke asked. He cast far into the slow-moving river. Sun sparkled on the ripples caused by the lure breaking the surface.

Silas pretended he hadn't heard. Taking the afternoon to go fishing might set him back a little on his projects but he needed to give his brain a rest. But that would only happen if Luke didn't pry into his current situation.

Leaning back in the boat, Luke gave him a long look. "That good, huh?"

"I know what you're asking," Silas said. He loved being on the river. It had been the only place he'd felt at peace when he was a teenager, no matter what else was happening in his life or what messes he'd made. For the first time, he didn't feel relaxed on the water. He felt tightly wound, unable to settle his thoughts. His stomach churned and his chest felt heavy. He hadn't slept well and he was simultaneously exhausted and too anxious to sleep.

"Okay, then how's Violet?"

Silas thought about ignoring Luke completely, or maybe mentioning how he'd almost broken Violet's nose, but he was too tired to play games. "Still hates my guts."

"I'm sure she doesn't—"

"No, pretty sure she does." Silas pulled the brim of his cap down over his eyes. "I think I can tell when a girl hates me. I'm not that dense."

Luke was quiet for a moment. "Maybe you should do something nice for her, like bring—"

"Bring her flowers? Yeah, I tried that." Silas was focusing on the river but he still saw Luke's surprised expression. "And a book I thought she'd like."

"She wouldn't take them?"

"No, she seemed happy." He closed his eyes, trying not to remember how hopeful he'd been for that single, shining moment.

"Then what went wrong?"

"No idea." He tried to make it sound like he didn't care but he heard the sadness in his own voice.

"Well, there must have been something. If she was happy with the flowers and the book, and then suddenly not happy with you, I'd say you probably said something wrong.

Did you mention—"

"You know what? I really don't want to talk about it so maybe just mind your own business," Silas snapped.

Luke was quiet for a moment. "Sure thing."

They sat in silence for several long minutes until Silas turned back to his friend. Luke had been one of the first people in town to welcome him home. He knew exactly the kind of person Silas had been, but he'd invited him to lunch. When most people held on a little tighter to their watches and wallets, Luke had made Silas feel welcomed.

"Sorry about that. I just feel so..." He didn't know what adjective to use. "I really want to make things different and I can't."

"You like her," Luke said quietly.

Silas glared at him, ready to blow his top again at the bizarre suggestion that he had a thing for Violet Tam. Sure, she was pretty and smart. And funny, when she wasn't spitting mad at him. "I hardly know her."

"You've known her most of your life. I think you've always liked her. People don't change that much."

"Then, by that argument, she's right to hate me. I was a jerk and I'd like to think I've changed just a little bit."

"You didn't deny it." Luke sounded pleased with himself.

Silas stared out at the river for a while. He didn't want

to look too closely at his feelings for Violet. He didn't believe in love at first sight, or whatever happened when two people fell in love within hours. But if it wasn't love at first sight, that meant he'd liked Violet when they were in school together.

"Come on. It's not that bad. You look like someone stole your dog," Luke said, trying to lighten the mood.

"I was just considering the options." Silas reeled in his line a little, still sorting out his thoughts. "If I do… like her, then maybe I always have."

Luke smiled at him as if that wasn't a terrible thing to say. "Unrequited love?"

"Not in a good way."

"What do you mean?" Luke asked.

"What kind of guy does that make me? I liked her and she rejected me, so I made her life miserable? What kind of guy does that?"

Luke reeled in his line and cast it again before answering. "Is that what happened?"

"No. Maybe. I don't think so." He shook his head. "It was a long time ago."

"So, let's not rush to conclusions. And does it matter why it happened?"

Silas shot him a look. "If you'd spent years harassing some poor girl in your class, you wouldn't think that the reason wasn't important."

Luke nodded. "You're right. I get it. I just think that if you want to move forward, you shouldn't spend so much time dwelling on something that happened ten years ago."

His line jerked and Silas yanked back on his pole. After reeling frantically for a few minutes, he lifted a rainbow trout out of the water and flipped it into the boat.

"Nice," Luke said, peering over his shoulder. "A good twenty inches, I'd say."

He unhooked the fish and felt a little of the morning's angst fade away. Maybe it was a cliché of the alpha male or the cave man need to hunt, but there was something very satisfying about landing a big fish. "You say rainbow trout. I say dinner."

"I guess no pizza for you, right?" Luke said, laughing.

Silas felt the smile slip from his lips. Even if he never went back to Fire and Brimstone for pizza, he would have to face Violet.

"Sorry," Luke said softly. "That came out wrong."

"It's fine," he said although it wasn't. Not at all. "The project should take about a week…" He suddenly remembered the butcher block areas in the kitchen that Mrs. Tam had requested. "And a half. Two at the most. It'll be fine."

"I'm sure it will." Luke was quiet for a moment. "If there's anything you need, just let me know."

There was nothing that anybody could do, but Silas appreciated the thought. "Thanks."

He cleared his throat. "How's Romy?"

There was something in Luke's tone that caught Silas's attention. An extra casualness that was unlike him. He thought back to all the times Romy and Luke had been in the same room. Nothing ever seemed out of the ordinary. But he knew when someone was acting too casual and there was always a reason for it. "She's sad. She's having a hard time adjusting. And she has this idea that she needs to harvest everything in the garden and put it up for the winter like our mom did."

"Can I help?"

Silas looked over at him. "You want to pick tomatoes and peppers?"

"Whatever she needs. You both need," he quickly corrected himself.

For a moment, Silas wanted to tell Luke there was really nothing he could do. Not because the garden was in such good shape, but because he couldn't imagine his little sister dating Luke.

It shouldn't have been such a surprise that Luke had a thing for Romy. His sister was beautiful and smart, plus she had a great sense of humor. Add in her many talents and it was more shocking that guys weren't knocking down the door. Or maybe they had been before their mom had passed away and Romy had put everything on hold while she cared for her. Silas realized he wasn't really sure what kind of social life Romy had

had before he'd moved back to town. He'd been so worried over facing the people that he'd hurt, he hadn't considered how moving in would affect Romy. He'd assumed it would be all good, but maybe she was dealing with more than just their mother's death. Maybe a lot of things had changed for her.

Silas felt a new wave of guilt. He was out on the river fishing while Romy did all the work on their little family farm. He'd been so wrapped up in his own problems that he'd forgotten his primary responsibility was to Romy now. Luke had reminded him of that. "We can head over later this afternoon, if you've got time. I know she was planning on making spaghetti sauce and salsa this week."

"Excellent," he said, grinning.

If it had been any other couple, Silas would have made a crack about how excited Luke was to pick produce in the hot afternoon sun. As it was, he said nothing. The idea would take some getting used to.

As Silas cast out into the river again, he felt more than a little jealousy at the idea of Luke and Romy. Not because he didn't think Luke was good enough, or that Romy shouldn't date, but because they were starting out fresh. There was no painful past and no present hurt feelings to keep them apart. Silas pulled the brim of his hat lower over his eyes again and wished for the thousandth time that he had never met Violet before moving back to Arcadia Valley.

"Mom, are you sure? I thought Demi was coming in the afternoons to help you and Elise as you guys worked straight through the week." Violet shifted the pile of cedar in her arms and frowned at her mother.

"I'm sure," she said, taking the bundle from Violet. "Demi's watching her granddaughter and Elise had an appointment. We worked from five this morning blanching tomatoes. I think that's a good day's work."

"Then you should go home to rest, not come here. Everything is fine." Violet tried to take back the wood.

Turning so it was out of her reach, she said, "I know it is. I have an ulterior motive for taking over." She peered at Violet. "Is that a black eye? Or is it make up?"

"It's a black eye," Jamie said from behind them. She was tying on her apron as she walked into the kitchen area. Violet hadn't realized how late it was but it was at least four thirty if Jamie was already there.

"Barely. Just a bruise, really." Violet shot Jamie a look that told her to be quiet but her friend went on.

"Silas gave it to her yesterday. She said her rear was really sore, too."

Her mother turned to her, eyes wide. "Explain. Now."

"Mom, it's nothing. We collided when I rushed around a corner. I fell pretty hard. He was sorry." She rubbed her face and then regretted it. Her nose was still sore, but Jamie was right. It was mostly her bottom that was in pain. As long as she didn't sit down, she was fine.

"Oh, so those flowers in the office are from him?" If anything, her mother looked even angrier.

"Flowers?" Jamie asked, a smile spreading over her face.

"Mom, please. It was nothing." Violet searched for some way to convince her mother. "Do you think Thor would let anybody hurt me? He's a sweet dog, but if anybody looked sideways at me, Thor would neutralize them in a second. Silas almost got bitten and it wasn't even his fault."

Her mother started to smile. "That's true. That dog is the best bodyguard around."

"So, what's this ulterior motive you mentioned?" Violet was relieved they could move on from Silas. Her crying jag in the office was fresh in her mind. Her attempt to get answers from him had turned into the world's most awkward confrontation. She wasn't going to speak to him unless she had to.

"I was going to manage things here while you go help out Romy in her garden."

Violet almost choked at the words. "Romy?"

"Sounds like you're being drafted," Jamie said, laughing.

"Actually, I was hoping I could draft you both together."

Violet had to smile a little. That was just like her mother. Not that she minded in the least. Her mother had always relied on her and she was happy to help out. It's what family did. Since she'd started teaching, her mother had acted as if Violet was almost a distant relative, not wanting to encroach on her time.

"So, what does Romy need?"

"You know Mary Black passed away. Well, Romy is struggling with the farm. She's done great taking over the cheese making, the milking, the animal care. But the garden is out of control, and now it's time to harvest some of the produce."

Violet tried to keep her expression neutral. She wondered if Silas had been talking to her mother. "How did you find out?"

"I called to check on her. She said she'd heard we were making the pizza sauce this week and offered me her mother's canning supplies. I asked her why she wasn't keeping it and…" Her mother paused. "I don't want to gossip but she had a bit of a meltdown."

Violet cringed. Romy was a strong person. It would take a lot to break her. She knew what it felt like to reach the end of your rope and have a good cry.

"Meltdown?" Jamie asked.

"Said she couldn't possibly do it all, even though she hated to not finish what her mother started in the spring. I convinced her that she'd feel better if she did at least a few jars, not trying to fill the basement shelves, but just a little bit. I think knowing she did something rather than nothing would be some comfort."

"What about her brother?" Violet asked, trying to sound casual.

Her mother cocked her head. "Silas? He's busy, too. He's got a lot of projects on his plate right now. It's probably not a priority to pick and can a bunch of tomatoes."

Violet felt shame for bringing him up. Of course he was busy. It's not like he had a summer break like a teacher.

"It would be awful to waste all that food," Jamie said. "Besides the fact her mom planted everything, it would just be sad to have so much rot on the vine."

Her mother nodded. "Exactly. And Mary was always so committed to eating locally, producing her own food and putting it up for winter. She influenced the whole direction of this restaurant. One day I said the grocery store peppers were a little old and she gave me a speech about supporting the farmers market. She's the one who first encouraged me to make our own sauce."

Violet saw tears glint in her mother's eyes. For the first time, she realized that hiring Silas to build a breakfast bar may not have been an entirely aesthetic choice. Perhaps if it had been her own mother who had died, Mary Black would have reached out in the same way and found some way to connect with Violet.

"I'm in," Jamie said, taking off the long white apron she had just tied around her waist. "Does she know we're coming, or should we just show up?"

"I'll give her a call. She was going to harvest and then can a little bit this afternoon." Violet's mother looked at her, black eyes assessing. She didn't say anything more, simply waited for her daughter to make a decision.

Silas certainly would never ask her to help, even if she had offered to help Romy. It was the right thing to do. "I hate to leave you short-handed."

Her mother winked, tucking the cedar under one arm. "Don't worry about us. The wait times might be a bit longer, but we'll survive. Romy is the one who needs some help. And really, just knowing that people care is important right now."

Jamie clapped her hands. "Awesome. As much I love slinging pizzas and flirting with the cute guys, I love the garden more. Let's go get dirty," she said.

110

"Right behind you." Violet took off her apron and folded it. Although she loved Jamie's enthusiasm, she couldn't help feeling a wave of anxiety. Just that morning she'd vowed to stay out of Silas's way. Now she was headed to his house to spend time with his sister. Maybe if they could get in and out without bumping into him, it would be okay.

As she gathered her keys and her purse, Violet tried not to worry. God knew what He was doing and surely he would never throw her into a situation that would cause her any more pain than she'd already endured. Violet would go to Romy's house and do her best to show the girl that people cared. And God would make sure Silas stayed away until they got most of the garden picked.

CHAPTER NINE

"I would feel more optimistic about a bright future for man if he spent less time proving that he can outwit Nature and more time tasting her sweetness and respecting her seniority."

— E.B. White

Romy Black brushed her dark hair from her eyes, making a dirt smudge across her forehead. The hundred year old but freshly painted yellow farmhouse stood behind her, a cheerful sign of Arcadia Valley's farming history. Violet paused, a tomato in hand, and thought how a picture of Romy at that moment would fit perfectly in a glossy calendar on country life. She was pretty in the way fresh-faced farm girls tended to be, with a tan that spoke of hours of work in the sun. Of course, Thor added the perfect touch to the scene as he sat quietly in the shade near the back steps.

Romy met her gaze and said, "Are you sure you're feeling okay to be out here?"

"Why? Oh, the eye." Violet touched her face. "It looks

worse than it is." She didn't mention her sore tailbone. It seemed like a topic best kept between close friends and she hardly knew the girl.

Romy seemed to accept that. "I can't thank you enough for—"

"Stop thanking us," Jamie said from her place a few feet away. "It's our pleasure."

"You're so bossy," Violet said. "Let her thank us if she wants." She straightened up and held up a green striped tomato. "I'm loving all of these different heirloom plants. We just have Romas and San Marzanos because of all the sauce we make. What do you make with these?"

"My mom…" Romy stopped for a moment, cleared her throat and went on. "My mom made salsa, relish, spicy tomato juice, you name it."

"What are you going to do with them?" Jamie lugged her bucket another few feet and reached into a caged tomato plan that stood taller than she did.

"I'm not sure yet. I'll probably share them, if anybody wants any. I have the recipes and the time, but it's just such a big job." Romy blinked back tears and she laughed softly. "Sorry. This garden just brings back so many memories. I don't mean to get all emotional."

"My turn to be bossy, I guess." Violet reached across the row and touched Romy's shoulder. "Don't apologize to us for missing her. And like Jamie said, it's our pleasure to help you out here. My mom hated the idea of you trying to harvest everything yourself." She wanted to make a pointed comment about filling in for missing siblings but she didn't dare.

As if she read Violet's thoughts, Romy said, "Silas called right before you two showed up. He and Luke should be here in a few minutes. They're just putting the boat away."

Violet froze. "Coming here?" she repeated.

"To help out. And he's picking up some meat at Deli's Sausages for dinner. You're staying for dinner, right?"

"If he didn't know we were coming, there won't be enough. We'll just head out as soon as we're done here." Something in her expression must have raised Romy's suspicions.

"There'll be plenty. They caught some nice fish, too. Are you worried about Loki? She's not territorial at all and wouldn't hurt a fly." Romy glanced back at Thor.

"No, she's great. And they already met." Violet shot a look at Jamie but her friend was halfway inside a tomato bush. Maybe they could quickly pick the rest of the garden and slip away before Silas showed up. Violet scanned the area and her heart sank. There was at least another two hours of work, not including washing or laying them out on a tarp.

Her mind raced, grabbing possible excuses and then discarding them. Violet looked down at her clothes, grimacing at the sight of her ragged T-shirt and cut-off jean shorts. She would have worn something without holes if she'd known they'd be entertaining. Ducking her head and searching for more tomatoes, Violet reminded herself that Silas lived there and if he came to work in his own garden, he was hardly required to give advance notice.

They worked in silence for a long while, moving buckets up and down the row. Violet felt the peace of the garden seep into her heart and her muscles relaxed, even as she used them to carry the heavy loads.

"There they are," Romy said, and Violet heard the smile in her voice.

She resisted looking up for as long as she could. Maybe if she just kept working, Silas would see her and decide to work on the other side of the farm. She'd seen plants dotted with brightly colored produce, probably peppers. Maybe Luke and Silas would just wave and move in that direction.

"Hi, everybody."

Violet tried not to sigh at the sound of Luke's voice. He was such a friendly guy. There was no way he would let Silas drag him past without saying hello. Now that she thought about it, Violet wondered why Luke was friends with Silas anyway. They were nothing alike.

"Hey," Jamie said. "Come on in and join the fun. Violet's got the extra buckets at the end of her row."

She had no option but straighten up and face them. The first thing she noticed was Silas's expression. Surprise, confusion, and something else she couldn't define. She'd probably wear the same expression if she came home to find Silas in *her* garden.

"How's your nose, Violet? I heard about your accident," Luke said as he walked toward them. "Or should I say your eye?"

"I'm fine," she said, and hated the shaky sound of her voice.

Luke peered at her face. "Did you go see a doctor?"

"No, it's really nothing. Just a bloody nose and a little bit of a black eye."

"You could have fractured a nasal or lacrimal bone. Or even the zygomatic arch."

Violet remembered that Luke was a pediatrician and for a moment, she worried that she'd been walking around with a skull fracture. "Wouldn't I know?"

"Not necessarily. But there's usually a lot more swelling at the site, so it's probably okay. And no headache or blurred vision? No trouble breathing or numbness?"

"No." Violet wondered what Luke would say if she asked how to treat a bruised tailbone. He'd probably give her lots of advice without even blinking. If they were alone, she might have asked. As it was, she was intensely aware of Silas just a few feet away. She cleared her throat and looked over at Thor. He was busy sniffing Loki and wagging his tail harder than he probably had in his whole life. "Just a little sore."

"Well, make sure to get some x-rays if you don't feel better or something changes. And Silas won't be running around corners anymore. Right, Silas?"

Silas didn't respond. He was looking at Romy, as if he wanted to ask her why she hadn't mentioned the guests in the garden. But then again, Romy wouldn't have known Violet and Jamie were coming. Violet felt a little bad for the girl, caught in the middle of an old feud that didn't seem to be ending anytime soon.

"So, what's the plan?" Silas asked, looking around. "Are we canning today?"

"No, there's not enough time for that. Mom always picked one day, and then canned the next. It's too much for one afternoon." Romy didn't seem irritated that her brother knew so little about the process.

Luke walked past Violet and grabbed two buckets. "I'll start at the other end and pick towards you guys."

"I'll go with you," Romy said. Violet wondered if it was her imagination or did she volunteer a little too quickly. Was she trying to get out of the way? Did she expect Silas and Violet to start arguing? She watched Romy walk with Luke to the far side of the garden and felt her face go warm with embarrassment. Whatever was between them, Romy certainly didn't need to be afraid of them making a scene. She was here to help, not to cause trouble.

"Is it okay if I go get a glass of water?" Jamie said, brushing off her hands.

"Of course. Help yourself to anything in the fridge," Silas said.

"Can I grab you guys something?"

"No, I'm okay," Violet said.

Silas shook his head. "No, nothing for me right now."

After Jamie had left the row, Violet put her head down and picked as if the only thing that mattered in the world was finding the most perfect tomato. She could hear Thor letting out deep, playful woofs and Loki answering him. It would have made her very happy if it had been anybody else's dog. She wondered if this is what a mother felt like when her kid made friends with her enemy's kid. Awkward.

They picked in silence for a while, Romy and Luke's conversation drifting over to them. Romy let out a laugh, and Violet looked over, suddenly understanding why she'd been so eager to leave their row.

"Oh," she said softly.

Silas followed her gaze to Romy and Luke. "Not sure how I feel about that," he said.

Violet was tempted to pretend she hadn't heard him,

but she'd never been very good at giving someone the silent treatment. "I thought you were friends."

"We are. Sort of makes it worse. I know him better than she does." He shrugged a little as if apologizing for being protective.

"He seems like a good guy," she said as she crouched beside a large plant and stretched her arm into the bush. She could see an enormous, orange tomato hanging like a mango in the shady interior.

"He is, really." Silas plucked the tomato from the other side and offered it to her.

"Thanks," she mumbled. It was hard enough to work side by side. She wished he would just focus on his own plants and not be so helpful.

"It just means he has a better chance."

"Isn't that a good thing?" Violet wasn't sure why she was still talking.

"I don't know if I'm ready for any more changes." He smiled at her, but it was a rueful sort of smile.

"Ah," she said and hauled her bucket to the next plant. She got it. She really did. As a grown woman with a good job, her own place, and her own friends, she should be secure enough to handle any kind of changes life threw her way. But Violet had always struggled with change. She'd recognized that fact about herself way back in college. Sometimes even the changing seasons made her a little sad. It was hard to say goodbye to something she loved, even if she knew something wonderful was coming. "But maybe it won't work out."

Silas glanced over at Luke and Romy. They were kneeling across from each other, talking as they picked. "No, it will. If it gets a chance."

"How do you know?"

"I just do." He looked at her. "Haven't you ever seen two people together and known they would fall in love?"

Violet stared into his eyes, trying to remember back through the years. She thought of all her friends who had become couples and gotten married. At this time in her life, she felt like every summer was filled with wedding after wedding, bridesmaid dress after bridesmaid dress. "I don't think so. You have?"

"Sure. It's just something about the way they look at each other, as if nobody else in the world matters."

She frowned at him. "Doesn't everyone act like that when they first meet someone they like?"

"Nope. Romy dated a guy last year and I knew it wouldn't work out. She liked him, but she wasn't..." He looked up at the sky, a tomato in one hand, searching for the right words. "Entranced. Sometimes he would say something and she'd miss it because my mom was talking or Loki was barking. But she never misses anything Luke says or does."

Violet looked past Silas toward the Luke and Romy. For just a moment, she wondered what it would like to feel that way. They were in the first stages of a relationship and they only had eyes for each other.

"Are— are you okay?" Silas asked.

She turned back to him, preparing to make some excuse for what must have shown on her face. But as she met his eyes, she felt her answer evaporate, and in its place a new response formed. "I'm just jealous. No big deal." She added a smile to soften her words.

His brows went up. "Jealous of Romy because of Luke?" His tone was casual.

Violet had to laugh a little at the idea of her fighting Romy for Luke. "No, not that way. Luke is great, but I've never thought of him like that."

Silas visibly relaxed. She imagined how awful it would have been for Silas to discover a love triangle brewing between his best friend, his sister, and the girl who couldn't stand him.

"Then what are you jealous of?"

"People in love. People wanting to be in love." She ducked her head and looked inside the shady interior of the plant. Her cheeks felt warm and she wished she hadn't said anything.

"Doesn't everybody want to be in love?" His voice was muffled. She could hear him tossing tomatoes into his bucket.

"Not me." She sounded confident in her answer but a sudden rush of doubt filled her. She lifted her bucket and walked a little away from him, giving herself space to think. She examined her heart, tried to call up her deepest wishes. In that moment, Violet realized that there was a bright line drawn across her life, a line that separated it into two separate parts: before Silas returned, and after.

Last year Violet had worried about her students' test scores, her mother opening a restaurant, and Thor getting enough exercise. The idea of falling in love with anybody hadn't really been on her radar. She'd thought it would happen sometime down the road, in a few years, when she was ready.

Now, she was fighting a rising tide that threatened to sweep her along with it, whether she wanted it or not. Silas had come back into her life with the same power he had wielded ten years ago.

"Oh, no." Silas grunted out the words and bolted past Violet, running toward the house.

She stood up in shock. Her gaze traveled beyond him to the house. She searched for Jamie, suddenly afraid that Thor or Loki were attacking. It made no sense, but animals were sometimes unpredictable.

Her heart jumped into her throat as she rushed after Silas, trying to see past his height, tripping repeatedly on the vines in the path.

She finally reached the gate and stopped suddenly, her mind struggling to understand what she was seeing. Jamie had walked out the back door and was standing on the porch, a hand to her mouth, laughter in her eyes. Thor and Loki were a few feet away, clearly having moved from puppy love to something more serious.

"Oh, no," she said, echoing his dismay. "She's not spayed?"

Silas turned back, concern on his face. "No. She had all her shots but I made an appointment next month for the spaying. What should we do? I didn't even think— I mean, don't dogs show signs of being in heat? She hasn't acted any differently."

Violet shook her head. "I've only had a boy dog. I think males can make puppies any time." It was like a train wreck. She wanted to look away but couldn't seem to make herself focus anywhere else. She certainly didn't want to look at Silas. And to think she'd been irritated that Thor and Loki had become *friends*. If only that had been the worst thing to happen. It looked like she had a lot more to worry about than Thor wanting to play with Loki at the park.

CHAPTER TEN

"The creation of a thousand forests is in one acorn."

— Ralph Waldo Emerson

Luke and Romy came to stand beside Violet. Romy giggled a little and then cleared her throat, as if trying not to act like a sixth grader. "I don't think you guys want to get in the middle of that. Better to just leave them alone. They're not mean, but if you try to force them apart, they might turn on you."

"Maybe they're just... having fun. Maybe it doesn't mean they'll have puppies." Violet wondered why she knew so little about dog breeding. She'd had Thor for years but had never taken the time to really learn about it. Having him neutered hadn't seemed a priority since he wasn't aggressive and didn't seem interested in other dogs. As she stared in shock at the scene before her, she realized how very stupid that had been.

Jamie very carefully walked around the dogs and joined them near the garden. "So, looks like you guys are going to be grandparents. Congratulations!"

Violet shot her a look. "Not funny."

"Too young to be a grandma, eh?" Luke was clearly finding it all very amusing. "I think a lot of parents feel that way. At least you got a heads up. Sometimes it comes as a total surprise."

"I just…" Silas shook his head, not seeming able to finish his sentence. "Puppies."

"Maybe," Violet added. "We don't know that."

"There are so many jokes I could be making right now," Luke said.

"And we all appreciate your self-control." Romy nudged him with her elbow.

Violet thought of how easily they touched each other and how comfortable they were trading barbs. She wondered what it would be like to fall in love with someone who was a friend first, before anything else. That was the best way. No drama, no tears.

"We should get back to work," Silas said. As Romy,

Jamie and Luke walked back into the garden, Silas gestured to Violet. She hung back.

"I'm sorry. If I had known they would—"

"Me, too. And you had no way of knowing. If anything, I should have gotten Thor fixed a long time ago. It just didn't seem necessary since he's so calm and he's not around many other dogs." For some reasons she could feel her face heating up and she glanced toward the garden. "I guess we'll wait and see what happens. Maybe it's nothing. Maybe it's just…" She didn't quite know how to end that sentence.

He cleared his throat. "Right. I wonder when we'll know."

Violet knew a lot about human biology but she had no idea how long it took for a dog to show. Or how they would find out before Loki started to get fat? "Do they do a blood test? Those can be expensive. I'll help with the cost, of course, since it's Thor's fault. Or my fault." She wanted to put her hands to her cheeks but she didn't. Maybe he would just think she was sunburned and overheating after all the work in the garden.

For the first time, Silas smiled. "I don't think it's always the guy's fault. I think they bear equal responsibility here."

"True. We should make them help pay for all the medical bills. Maybe Thor can get an after school job and Loki can help out in your shop."

"Tough love," Silas said. "I approve."

"But whatever happens, we'll love and welcome the grandbabies," Violet said. She was trying hard to make light of the situation but she wasn't laughing inside. She really didn't want to be dealing with a batch of puppies and was hoping they wouldn't need to split any costs at all. They'd just go on as before. Acquaintances. No real connection besides the past.

They stood there smiling at each other for a few moments. Loki wandered into their line of sight and they both turned. "I'm going to take her inside now," Silas said.

Violet nodded as he moved away, but then reached out on a whim. She meant to get his attention, as he had gotten hers just a few minutes before, but instead touched his arm. He froze, eyes questioning.

"I really could have prevented this by being a more responsible pet owner. Thanks for not making this all my fault."

He shook his head. "We're equally to blame. Really. No apology necessary. I guess it's one of those things we should have talked about when they first met. I don't know why I didn't think of it."

As he walked away, Violet thought back to that first day at Fire and Brimstone. She knew why she hadn't thought to ask if Loki was fixed. She'd been so consumed by her own anxiety and worries that there hadn't been room for anything else. Maybe there was a message there for her. Maybe the bad memories she carried around were skewing her judgment in more ways than she realized. Maybe it was affecting a lot of areas in her life that needed perspective.

Picking up an empty bucket, Violet resolved to be more focused. And she couldn't help adding a desperate prayer that there would be no puppies. *Please, please, please.* She didn't want to be attached in any way to Silas for the next few months. Or for any length of time at all. One week was hard enough to get through as she felt the layers of pain and bad history peel back like onion skin, exposing the tenderness beneath. With each encounter, she was more and more vulnerable, and unsure.

Only a few more days and they could return to their separate circles. It was possible to live in Arcadia Valley without seeing each other too often, she was sure of it. And if it didn't happen naturally, she'd make sure to avoid him on purpose. She was a good Christian but God didn't say anything about being friends with an enemy. He said to love them, and she was sure she could do that by wishing Silas well from far away.

Silas took Loki inside and told her to lie down on her dog bed. She lifted big brown eyes and let out a soft woof that said she knew she was being punished, but didn't know why.

He sighed and reached out to give her a nice scratch behind the ears. "Not your fault, girl. It's all on me. I got distracted. Just wasn't thinking."

Loki wiggled closer and bumped her head against his hand. She didn't like to see him upset. That was one of the first things Silas had noticed about Loki. She could read his moods better than Romy or Luke or even his mother when she was alive. Loki could sense anxiety or worry, and she pushed her big body against his leg or nudged his hand with her head. It was as if she wanted to remind him that love existed, that all was not lost.

And it was true. All was not lost. But it certainly felt like it was sliding down a steep slope, heading for a drop off that would throw him into a ravine. Silas knelt down and let Loki put her head on his shoulder.

"Don't worry. We'll figure it out." He knew she couldn't understand him and she didn't really care, anyway. Of course Loki would care for her puppies and didn't mind if she was connected to Violet in any way, but Silas imagined months of sharing vet visits and puppy care with Violet, and his heart dropped. He was barely holding on as it was. Just being around her took more strength than he felt he had. If they could just interact like normal people, everything would be fine, but it seemed they were destined for drama. It seemed every conversation ended with his heart in throat and his hands shaking from nerves. This was probably the first time they had parted amicably. Or almost amicably. He could tell she was incredibly embarrassed and felt the dogs' misbehavior was all her fault. It was really more of a truce than a friendly encounter.

Standing up, he gave Loki one last pat and headed for the back door. As he entered the kitchen, Romy walked in.

"Hey, we made good time with the picking. Want to start up the grill?" She scrubbed her hands at the sink. "I wish I could jump in the shower really fast. You couldn't hold down the fort while I got cleaned up, could you?"

"Sure." Silas wanted to remind Romy that she'd never felt the need to get dressed up for a simple barbeque before. Something had changed and he didn't even know when it had happened, but he knew Luke was the reason she didn't want to sit around in sweaty clothes with dirt on her face. "Are Jamie and Violet staying?"

She turned and gave him a look. "Why did you say it that way?"

"What way?" He heard the defensiveness in his voice.

"Like you don't want them to stay."

He took his turn at the sink. "No idea what you're

talking about."

Romy leaned against the sink, trying to get him to look at her. "Silas, you can't lie to me."

He turned away and wiped his hands on a towel. "How could a question be a lie?"

"Huh. I don't know the answer to that but I do know you sounded weird right then. Whatever problem you have with them, you need to get over it because they just spent the last few hours picking our tomatoes in the hot afternoon sun. They deserve a cold pop and some good grilled sausages."

"I have no problem with anybody." He didn't look her in the eyes.

"What happened between you and Violet?"

He looked at her then, trying to ferret out information from her expression. "Why do you ask? You mean the black eye? That was an accident."

Romy fixed him with a long look. "You've never been one to talk a lot to me about what you're thinking, but I was hoping you'd be more open now that now that we're the only two left."

Romy was right. Now that their mother was gone, they needed to stay close, just as she'd have wanted them to be. His first instinct was always to keep his thoughts and fears inside, but she and Luke were his closest friends. He shouldn't carry every burden alone. "I wasn't very nice to Violet in high school."

"In high school? That was a long time ago."

"It wasn't just normal teasing. I was mean. She hated me." He held up a hand. "And before you say she needs to get over it, you should know that I'm completely on her side."

Romy shook her head. "Which is what? I don't understand what's going on. If she hated you, she wouldn't be here. She wouldn't talk to you or even give you the time of day. So, there must be something more going on here."

He tried to think of a way to explain but realized that even if he repeated their conversations verbatim, it would never fully illuminate everything in his heart. "It's just that we seemed to be— that maybe we could have—" No, she never wanted to accept his apology. "We weren't going to be friends, ever, but I was hoping to say I was sorry."

Romy frowned. "And why can't you?"

"I tried. She didn't want to hear it."

"When? Today?"

He thought of their first meeting and felt a second wave of shame. "No, a few weeks ago. We ran into each other at Fire and Brimstone. I started to apologize but she shut me down."

Romy's mouth made a little 'o' shape. "I think I got it now. You tried to make up to her the first time you exchanged words, probably in front of a bunch of people and she brushed you off."

"Not a bunch," he protested.

"And you haven't tried since because you know she hates your guts."

"Pretty much."

Romy heaved a sigh that said she thought her brother was a few sandwiches short of a picnic.

"It's not just that. We've tried…" He rubbed a hand over his face. Violet had tried. He had stood there sweating until she'd run off to the office. "Okay, so maybe there's a chance now that we've had a little more time together. But giving her a black eye didn't help much."

"Well, now that you're going to have puppies together, you'll have a lot more time to get to know each other better." Romy laughed as she headed for the bathroom.

Silas rolled his eyes. "I'll go out and keep everyone occupied while you get fancied up for Luke."

He heard her faint squawk of protest but didn't pause on his way out the door. Stomping down the porch steps, he headed for the barbeque pit. Luke was already cleaning the grill and fresh mesquite wood chips were stacked in a small mound. They had cooked dinner outside enough times together that Luke was familiar with the process. Although Silas knew the Delis family preferred spit roasting for gatherings, Luke loved a simple backyard barbeque as much as the next guy.

"Anything we can do to help?" Jamie asked. "I don't feel very useful over here." She was stretched out in the hammock, a cold drink in resting on her stomach.

"Nope. We have it under control," Luke said, smiling over at her. "Maybe Romy needs help inside."

"She's taking a shower." She really had looked fine. There was no reason to get dressed up. Nobody was really that dirty. He glanced at Violet sitting beside Jamie, noting how she'd taken off her shoes and was wiggling her toes in the cool grass. With her cut off jean shorts, old T-shirt and hair swept back from her face, she was clearly comfortable as she was. She didn't need to dress up. She clearly didn't care. There was no reason to get fancy for a relaxed outdoor meal with friends after working in the garden.

For just a moment, Silas wished Violet did care. He wanted her to think of him the way Romy thought of Luke.

Violet looked up and met his eyes. Her expression changed from thoughtful to wary, then a question crossed her face.

He forced a smile and turned back to Luke, silently berating himself for being a fool. Apparently he was one of those guys who only wanted what he couldn't have. What was wrong with him? Allowing himself to develop some kind of crush on her wouldn't be fair to either of them and would only end in disaster.

♥♥♥♥♥

Violet focused on her bare toes in the lush green grass and tried to calm her pounding heart. The look on Silas's face had shaken her to the core. Wistfulness, yearning, misery. For the first time she wondered if there was more to his friendly overtures than wanting to apologize for his teenage behavior.

And if so, how did she feel? It was a question she didn't need to dwell on, because she already knew the answer. A hundred small moments over the past week slid into one undeniable feeling. Somehow, Silas had become much more than her tormentor from the past.

CHAPTER ELEVEN

"Should you shield the canyons from the windstorms you would

never see

the true beauty of their carvings."

— Elisabeth Kübler-Ross

"It was nice of you to stop by." Silas walked Ron Taylor back through the shop, trying not to see the piles of sawdust he hadn't cleaned up from that morning's work. Loki trotted at his side, bumping her head against Silas's hand, as if she was hoping they were headed to the truck.

"Thanks for letting me drop in. I just wanted to see where you made that beautiful gun cabinet. It's a work of art," Ron said. He looked like a country version of Santa Claus: white beard, twinkling blue eyes and plaid shirt.

"Thank you," Silas said. He'd never been good with compliments but it was nice when someone appreciated his work. They walked past Fire and Brimstone's new counter. It gleamed dully in the bright sunlight shining through the work space, ready for its first coat of lacquer. It was one of his best pieces but Silas felt a dull sense of unease every time he looked at it. Tomorrow he and a few helpers would haul it to the restaurant bright and early for its first fitting. Silas didn't know if he was feeling anxious about seeing Violet again, or that his week with her was coming to an end.

"My buddy Gil is gonna call you. He wants something like it, but to go around his wine cellar," Ron said, pausing at the front door. He hooked his thumbs in his belt loops and rocked back on his heels.

"An entire wine cellar?" Silas asked, trying to imagine what kind of process that would be.

"Just one of the little ones. You know, 'bout this high." He held a hand up to his waist. "Goes along the wall in the kitchen. Real nice cooling systems but they're usually stainless steel. Kind of an eyesore."

He smiled, enjoying the fact he lived in the sort of place that considered stainless steel unattractive. Not a lot of people enjoyed natural wood and even fewer liked reclaimed or salvaged materials. "I appreciate you spreading the word about the business. It means a lot. Especially after I stole from you."

"Now hear this, son." Ron looked stern. "Good judgment comes from experience, and a lotta that comes from bad judgment. You've got your head on straight now. Anyway, thanks for giving me the tour. It does my heart good to see your work. You've got real talent."

"Work I wouldn't be able to do without my internship, and that came from your letter of recommendation," Silas said.

"Oh, no way." He let out a low chuckle. "One little letter didn't change anybody's mind."

Silas didn't argue the point but he knew it helped to have a letter from the man who had pressed burglary charges on him as a teen. The master carpenter had given him a chance that he might not have otherwise. Silas had never hid his years in juvenile detention, but being honest had its drawbacks, like not being considered for any position that involved handling business contracts. Ron had stepped into the gap for him and Silas would never forget it. "Still, I appreciate it."

"I'm glad you asked, son. I always believed you'd straighten out. Some people just need a wake-up call."

Silas felt a surge of regret that it had taken years for him to answer that call, years that his mother had prayed and worried and waited. "And some people never do need that wake up call."

"Maybe." Ron considered that for a moment. "I think everybody's gotta have that moment when they realize they're on the wrong track. It's part of growing up. Sometimes it happens when you're young. Sometimes it happens a lot later.

What matters is that you listen and correct your course." He shrugged. "Listen to me. A Christmas tree farm philosopher."

"Pretty good advice to me." Silas glanced around. "Well, I'd better get this place cleaned up before I put on the lacquer."

"Right, I'll let you get to it. You're coming to dinner tonight at Elise's, right? I'm bringing corn on the cob and a watermelon."

"I sure am. I haven't decided what to bring yet but it better be good to keep up with her cooking."

Ron snapped his fingers. "Oh, I forgot to tell you. It's been moved to the Tam's place. Elise and Mrs. Delis are over there helping with the pizza sauce canning, and they thought it would be easier if we all just met there."

Silas blinked. He'd accepted Elise Camden's dinner invitation because he thought it would be an outdoor summer meal at her old farmhouse, a few older people around the table and low key atmosphere. Everything changed when he pictured himself at Mrs. Tam's for dinner. Then he remembered that Violet was working at the restaurant until late. It wasn't likely that she'd come home while he was there. Still, he'd make sure he was gone by the time the sun went down. He needed to be at Fire and Brimstone by five anyway. "Sure, that makes sense."

Ron gave him a curious look. "You get along okay with

them?"

He hesitated, not sure how to answer the question. Violet didn't get along with him, that was for sure. "Violet and I… We got off to a rocky start."

Grinning, he clapped Silas on the arm. "Same thing with me and Elise. We sure butted heads right from the start. Took us a long time to get past all the hurt and admit what we wanted. You'll find your way." He stepped through the door. "Well, see you tonight."

Silas lifted a hand and watched him walk toward his truck. His mind was still running to catch up with the idea of little white-haired widow Elise Camden and the old burly Christmas tree farmer together. Silas smiled as he closed the door behind Ron. People liked to say God works in mysterious ways. He supposed that was proof right there.

Violet hoped her first impression of the new server wasn't correct but the red-haired teen seemed a little too confident. Although she was friendly enough, Bernadette didn't seem like she was a very good listener and waitresses had to hone that skill, or the whole restaurant would suffer.

"The shift schedule is posted on the wall in the hallway

next to the office every Friday," Violet said.

"Okay." Bernadette fidgeted with her apron and gazed out at the tables as if unable to focus on what Violet was saying. Her large green eyes were rimmed with eyeliner and a tattoo peeped out of the edge of her blouse. "So, I don't work in the office at all?" she asked. "I'm good with numbers. You can ask Silas. He'll tell you."

"Silas?"

"Yeah, he's a friend of mine. He told me you guys needed help." She straightened her shoulders and Violet had the impression she was trying to appear older. "I used to make the deposits at my old job. It's not a problem."

"Uh, no. Thanks, but we've got that covered." Violet wondered how the girl had answered all the interview questions about waitressing but then thought she'd be doing bookkeeping and bank runs.

"Well, if you need me, I can do it. After hours, or whatever."

Violet nodded. "Thanks, but my mom usually handles all of that."

"Is she here?" Bernadette looked around.

"No, she's putting up the pizza sauce this week. I'm managing the restaurant for her and then I'll go back to teaching."

"So, you don't like working here? Silas told me you're a

teacher. I bet you hate having to deal with all this stuff."

Violet felt a flash of irritation. The girl was asking irrelevant questions while patrons were streaming through the door. "I like it. But it's not my job. Now, let's talk about serving. I know you've seen a few servers taking orders without their note pads but I'd like you to write everything down for a while. When you input the orders on the tablet, it shows up in the kitchen. I know it might seem like overkill, but getting an order wrong is a pain for everybody," Violet said.

"I guess. But I worked in a doughnut shop for months. I have a great memory." Bernadette crossed her arms over her chest but still didn't meet her eyes. Now she was focused on the hostess at the front of the restaurant.

Violet decided not to point out how getting a doughnut order wrong was different from having to rush a fresh pizza out to a hungry crowd of friends who had every order but one.

"Just use the notepad for a while. I trust you have a wonderful memory and nothing will ever go wrong. But just in the beginning, I'd like you to use the paper version and then input it." She softened her words with a smile. She really didn't envy her mother this part of the job. Somehow working with children was so much easier than working with adults. Or almost adults.

Violet looked up to see her mother had slipping in the side door and surveying the busy space. A smile touched Mrs.

Tam's lips as she saw the ovens crowded with pizzas and the tables filled. Cooks slid freshly made pizza pies onto serving platters with practiced ease. The lunch time crowd had them hopping, even with the recent hires. She met Violet's gaze and waved.

"If you need anything, let me or Jamie know. I'm going to go talk to my mom." Violet waited for a response but Bernadette walked toward the register where several servers where gathered. For a girl who had just been asking about the owner, she certainly didn't seem very interested in meeting her now. Sighing softly, Violet wondered if she had been as rude when she was young. She didn't think so. Especially to an employer. But maybe there was nothing to it. Bernadette may just not know how to communicate in the workplace. Lots of kids were more comfortable with people their own age and didn't know how to have a conversation with someone else. Just making eye contact was a good start, though.

Her mother started talking as soon as Violet was in ear shot. "We're canning the last batch of sauce today. You've done a great job running the place. Not a single complaint, the servers loved you, and business went up. Are you sure you guys don't want to stay on full time?" She winked but Violet could tell she was partly serious.

"I think one week was enough." She loved teaching eighth graders, but she really didn't mind helping out at the restaurant. Her extroverted personality was a good fit for that kind of job. She loved seeing people from all over Arcadia Valley trying out pizza with kimchi or speculating on what that certain flavor was in the sauce. One woman even offered her money to divulge the secret. Violet had smilingly declined because she'd known that even if the woman had added the required touch of Korean red chili flakes, it wouldn't have been the same. The days of slow cooking and home grown tomato crop made all the difference.

"Of course, we're going to work on sun drying the tomatoes and bottling them in olive oil this weekend. It might go on a little more than a few days. Maybe until next Wednesday."

"Wait. What?"

"You don't mind, do you?" She said it all very casually but Violet could tell she was invested in Violet's answer.

"Mom, what's going on? Just tell me straight out."

"Why would anything be going on?" She waved at an older couple being seated before turning back to Violet. "Unless you've had enough of the restaurant…"

"No, that's not it." Violet took a moment to regroup. Something was up but she couldn't really pin down how she knew. Her mother had never asked her to help out before and now she was extending her days at the restaurant like it was nothing. Very suspicious. "Of course I'm really happy to help out. Everyone has been great and I like getting to see people that I wouldn't otherwise."

"Good," she said, clapping her hands. "Silas and a few workers are installing the bar tomorrow morning around five. I'm afraid I have to take Elise to Twin Falls for an appointment so if you wouldn't mind, maybe you could be here. Just bring one of those mysteries you like to read if you don't have anything to do. It'll help pass the time."

Violet cocked her head. "Okay," she said slowly. "I guess I can be here. I don't have any plans tonight. I was just going to read and get to bed early. But don't you think he seems trustworthy? I don't think there would be any problem with just giving him the code for the door."

For a moment, Violet's mother looked like she was at a loss. "No, you're right. I do trust him. I just think it's better if somebody is here. And you're a morning person. You don't mind, do you? Bring Thor. Maybe he and Loki can have a playdate while Silas puts everything together."

Violet sighed, deciding not to explain how she wished Loki and Thor had remained unacquainted. "No, I don't mind."

"Now, I know it's not good to mix business with friendship, but I've invited him and a few friends over for dinner tonight and I was hoping you would come."

"Dinner tonight?" Her mind raced with possible

excuses. She's just told her mother she was available at five in the morning tomorrow because she had no plans. "What about the restaurant?"

"The assistant manager can take over for one evening. I thought you'd appreciate a day off and not one where you had to cook."

Violet searched for some reason she couldn't go but couldn't bring herself to lie. She could simply decline but then she'd have to explain why. There was no reason not to have a simple dinner with her mother and some friends.

"Sure, I can be there." Violet tried to sound a little more enthusiastic about getting a night off. "I'll probably bring Thor because he's been alone all day."

"Of course," her mother said, putting her arm. "The more the merrier."

Violet forced a smile but was thinking how it really wasn't an iron-clad rule. In fact, sometimes just a few people were the right amount. But bringing it up would only raise her mother's suspicions. They were hospitable, welcoming people who loved their community, and most dinners had two or three extra guests. It wouldn't make sense for Violet to start wishing for more time alone with her mother.

As she watched her walked toward the kitchen to chat with the cooks, Violet let out a small sigh. Maybe if she had been honest all those years ago, she wouldn't be shoved in

Silas's way so much. Maybe if she had been brave enough to share what was happening at school then she could have transferred earlier and avoided most of the pain. But maybes didn't save the world and she needed to take responsibility for her life right now. That also included facing the feelings she had for one dark-haired carpenter. She couldn't seem to shut him out of her life, no matter how hard she tried.

CHAPTER TWELVE

"I'd rather have roses on my table than diamonds on my neck."

— Emma Goldman

Silas stepped into Page Turners and felt himself automatically relax at the smell of books. He was a carpenter and was most at home working with wood, but books were a close second. Simply the sight of the packed shelves made him smile.

Irene, the owner, was at the front desk and they exchanged friendly waves. "I've only got about fifteen minutes to find a book," he called over to her.

"Or two," Irene said with a knowing look.

Her niece, Kenia, looked up from where she was opening a box and flashed a smile. "Or three," she said.

"You know me so well." Silas turned toward his favorite aisle, feeling the warmth of belonging to a community large enough to have a little privacy, but small enough that the bookstore owners knew your reading habits.

That feeling of warmth turned to surprise as someone walked directly into Violet Tam. He managed to check his speed the second before they made contact so instead of knocking her backward onto the hard floor, he merely pushed her off balance. She let out a grunt of surprise and dropped the book in her hands. Gripping her arms, he struggled to avoid stepping on her feet.

"I'm so sorry," he said. Just his luck that the moment he got close to her again, he'd run her over like a raging bull.

She looked up at him and laughed softly. "We've got to stop meeting this way."

Was she *flirting* with him? His face went hot. He wanted her to be flirting with him but it seemed so unlikely. It was much more likely to be her dry sense of humor rather than any romantic overture. "In the mystery aisle?"

"Around corners."

He tried to think of a witty response but his brain seemed to have shifted into neutral. Letting go of her arms, he bent down and picked up her book. He glanced at the cover before handing it to her.

"You're a Dennis Lehane fan?"

"I think so."

"You're not sure?"

"I read a few of his short stories and really liked them. Animal Rescue was great. I'm just not sure if his books are as good, but I'm willing to give them a try." She shot him a look. "At this point, most people say how much they liked Shutter

Island and ask me whether I thought Leonardo DiCaprio was great."

"Well, I can if you want," he said, trying not to smile. Taking off his cowboy hat, he ran a hand through his hair, wishing he hadn't come straight from the workshop and wasn't covered in sawdust. They not only had a shared love for the mystery genre, they seemed to agree that the movie was never as good as the book. "But do you know why Dennis Lehane doesn't write the screenplays the movie adaptations?"

She shook her head.

"He said he has no desire to perform surgery on his own child."

She laughed and Silas felt a surge of happiness at the sound. He'd just told Irene that he only had a few minutes to find a book, but he was mentally erasing that statement and hoping their impromptu meeting would turn into a long talk covering all things literary and perhaps a few subjects not found in the mystery section.

Her cheeks went pink. "I'd better go. I'm on a quick break from the restaurant."

"Of course, sure." He wanted to kick himself. He'd been standing there, smiling at her like he had straw for brains. "Me, too. I mean, I'm not on a break from the restaurant. But I've gotta get back to work."

Her lips twitched as if she was trying hard not to laugh.

"I'll see you later tonight."

"Yeah. Tonight." He stepped to the side so she could pass. "Wait… tonight?"

She paused, inches away from him. Looking up, her dark eyes were filled with some emotion he was afraid to name. "Dinner tonight. At my mom's house."

"You'll be there?" The moment the words left his mouth, he wanted to take them back. It sounded like he only accepted the invitation because he thought she'd be working.

"Yes. Is that a good or a bad thing?" She put a hand on her hip, her posture giving sass to her words, but there was a definite note of uncertainty in her voice.

"Good," he said hurriedly. "Definitely good." A long moment stretched between them as he saw the sass leave her expression and she looked at him with a vulnerability that made his chest tight.

"I— I should buy this." She held up her book and stepped away from him.

"Yeah, I should go, too." He started to follow her out of the aisle.

"Aren't you going to look for a book?"

"Right." He shook his head. "Book."

She pressed her lips together as if to keep from laughing. "See you."

He nodded and turned toward the rows of books. Her

footsteps faded away and the faint sound of voices echoed from the front of the store. Silas leaned his forehead against the shelf and closed his eyes. He couldn't have a conversation with Violet that didn't involve him making multiple inane statements and then losing his reason. She must think he was battling early onset dementia. Maybe she would even tell her mother that he shouldn't be putting in the new counter bar. As air-headed as he sounded around Violet, she might expect the thing to fall over at the first nudge.

Plucking a book from the shelf, he tried to read the back cover and couldn't focus on the words. He'd walked into Page Turners looking for something to read and now all he could do was replay their conversation over and over in his head. No one else had the ability to turn his day upside down faster than Violet, and there was nothing he could do about it. Maybe there had been some moment in the past few weeks where he'd knowingly stepped into the position he was in, but Silas couldn't think of one. It had all happened without fanfare, and now his heart was making decisions without his input.

Of all the things he'd expected to happen when he'd decided to return to Arcadia Valley, falling for Violet Tam was never one of them.

Violet opened the door and smiled. "Hi," she said, her voice a little too cheerful. She was wearing a flowered button up shirt with a flowing skirt that reached her ankles. Silas thought about how beautiful and at ease she looked, just as she had in the garden and at the bookstore. The girl could wear anything and look perfectly beautiful. One eyebrow arched and Silas quickly refocused.

The light yellow walls and white trim seemed to glow in the afternoon sun that shone through the windows. It was a classic farmhouse sitting room with a fireplace at one end and a piano at the other. He wondered if Violet played. A row of bookshelves was packed with books, classic and modern mixed together like spare socks in a basket. Silas wanted to go check the titles but he resisted. Looking around the empty living room, he said, "Am I early? I thought Ron said six. I can come back later."

"No, come on in." She waved him through the door way and he let the screen door shut with a soft thump. "I've been kicked out of the kitchen so you can keep me company in my exile."

"Romy sends her regrets. She and Charlotte, Nico's girlfriend, are going full power on the canning this evening." He held out a small bowl and a foil covered pan. For some reason, he suddenly felt shy.

Violet accepted them with a smile. She looked into the

bowl. "Carrot salad?"

"One of my mom's favorite recipes. Warm ginger carrot salad."

Pulling up a corner of the foil, she inhaled deeply. "These rolls smell amazing. Oregano, thyme…" She shook her head. "I can't name the rest."

"They're savory squash rolls. We had a lot of pumpkin and squash last year so we still had some puree in the freezer. The herbs and sharp cheddar seem to work together." He reached over and pulled out a roll, offering it to her. Even Romy had been impressed by how perfectly they had risen and browned this time.

Violet took a small bite and smiled as she chewed. "Romy is a genius."

For a moment, he wasn't sure whether to correct her or not. "These are mine, actually."

Her eyes went wide. "Is there anything you can't do?"

Silas gave her a long look. He didn't think she was being sarcastic. That wasn't really Violet's way. Realizing she was being sincere, he couldn't think of a response. She sounded as if he impressed her with all of his skills, when in reality he was simply a carpenter who knew a few good recipes.

Thor bounded through the room and stopped in front of Silas, sniffing his hand and giving an expectant look at the door. "Sorry, buddy. I left your new friend at home."

Violet cleared her throat. "So, any sign of…?"

"Well, she's been craving pickles and ice cream but from what I've been reading, it's too soon to tell. Maybe in a few weeks."

"A few weeks what?" Mrs. Tam asked as she entered the room, wiping her hands on a dishtowel.

Silas looked at Violet and an unspoken agreement passed between them. "Oh, nothing interesting." He smiled to soften his non answer. "Are you sure we can't help out in the kitchen?"

"No, we're almost ready." She looked at the dishes in Violet's hands. "You didn't have to bring anything."

"I know. But I don't usually get to cook for anybody other than Romy, and she's a better cook than I am."

"I know just how you feel," Violet said, laughing. "Everything I can make is just a pale shadow of the dishes my mother taught me."

He met her gaze and realized it was the second time in just a few minutes that she had treated him like a friend instead of an old enemy. Hope rose in his chest faster than he could fight it. He was afraid to give words to his yearning, but it was there, sharp and sweet. As many times as he'd tried to convince himself that it was an impossible task, his heart couldn't let go of the desire to somehow, in some way, make amends with Violet.

"There's my boy," Elise said. She was wearing a stained apron and had a pot holder in one hand. "You're sitting with me at church on Sunday again, right?"

Silas let himself be hugged and answered when he was let go. "Of course. I feel more comfortable at that service. My mom always went to the eight o'clock and it just…"

"Reminds you of her," Elise finished for him. She sighed. "Maybe in time you'll find some comfort in those things but I understand how hard it can be. When my husband passed away, I thought I might have to move. So many memories."

Mrs. Tam rubbed Elise's shoulder and smiled. "I'm glad you didn't. And I know Ron is, too."

Silas saw the moment Violet puzzled out that comment and almost laughed at her expression. It was probably the same one he had worn earlier that day.

"And speaking of Ron," Mrs. Tam said, nodding at the front door. Elise stepped forward to open the screen, a huge smile on her face. The paleness of her cheeks lessened a little as she waited for Ron to climb the porch steps.

"You didn't have to bring anything," Elise scolded him as he handed her a beautiful pie.

"I know, but I had a hankering for apple pie and thought I'd better bring it to share, or I'll undo all my healthy eating for the week." He kissed Elise on the cheek. "It's a selfish reason, but I'm a selfish man."

"Oh, you." She playfully swatted him on the arm and ushered him through the doorway.

"Is everyone here?" he asked.

"Demi decided to go home. She was saying that Charlotte and Nico don't go out very much, and I said that she should go offer to babysit little Elena. I know Charlotte loves that little girl, but every couple needs some time alone." Mrs. Tam chuckled and said, "And some need chaperoning."

Silas frowned, thinking that Mrs. Tam was suggesting that he wasn't to be trusted around Violet. He couldn't argue with the fact that he had bullied her in high school, but he hoped he could be trusted to behave himself around her now, even as beautiful as she was. He wasn't a predator. Then as Elise giggled, the realization hit him that Mrs. Tam was referring to Ron and Elise, and he almost laughed out loud.

Violet met Silas's gaze and this time her expression was a mix of horror and amusement. He wiggled his eyebrows at her and she turned away to stifle her laughter. There it was again— they were like friends, instead of enemies. Silas's heart needed only the smallest spark. Love bloomed inside him like a firework, lighting him up from the inside. He struggled to hide his emotion, thankful that Violet had stepped away.

"Shirley, you forget that I have my own house. I don't need you chaperoning my dinner dates." The laughter in Elise's voice belied her words.

"Well, that's my cue to exit the conversation," Violet said. "Plus, I still haven't shucked the corn."

"Let me help," Ron said, moving to follow her.

"No, Silas can go. You and Elise can bring the pie into the kitchen," Mrs. Tam said with a sly smile.

"First you want us apart, and now you want us together," Elise said. "I'm getting confused."

"Oh, you guys," Violet said, laughing. Silas could tell she was simultaneously embarrassed and charmed by the teasing of the older couple. "Come on, Silas. Let's go shuck corn."

He followed her willingly but Thor inserted himself between them, pausing for a moment to shoot Silas a look that said he was watching the man who had once given Violet a black eye. Silas tried to look meek and harmless but he wasn't sure if Thor was convinced. They passed through the airy kitchen and out onto the back porch. The large garden grew all the way to the path, leaving just a small strip of grass.

Thor bounded off the steps and went to sniff the rose bushes that lined the fence. Violet sat in front of a large bucket of corn and offered him an ear. She whispered softly, "Wow, that's a shocker. Did you know?"

Silas didn't need to ask her what she meant. "Just found out today. I think my jaw might have dropped."

She grinned as she stripped the leaves away. "Not to be ageist, but I just didn't even consider the possibility of them falling in love. I mean, she must be at least seventy five."

"I know. You're sort of expecting it when two young people spend time together, but…" His words trailed away. They were young and spending time together. He cleared his throat. "They probably have a lot in common. Known each other for years. Old friends." He was talking too fast.

Violet frowned into the bucket as she selected another ear. "They're on the library board together but I wouldn't have called them friends. In fact, I got the impression they didn't really like each other. Once I saw them have an argument over whether electric cars would ever be a viable option for a farming community. It got pretty heated."

"Maybe they were just intellectual disagreements and they got along as, you know, people." He felt his face starting to warm. *As people?* He sounded like an idiot.

"I guess, but even that way, I never saw them hang out together like some folks do. Sometimes I think I see the same group of old people everywhere I go, Demi's Delights, farmers market, Gas N Shop, Page Turners. I just never got the impression they could stand each other." She reached for another ear of corn.

"Mr. Camden didn't pass away until this year. Maybe they knew there was an attraction there but avoided each other.

Or maybe it's sort of a love-hate thing. All that animosity turned to passion. They say it's two sides of the same coin." Silas examined the kernels for strings of silk.

Violet didn't say anything for a moment. "I guess," she said softly.

He looked up, suddenly feeling the atmosphere had changed. He hadn't meant his words to be directed at her, but now that he replayed them in his head, it sure sounded as if he hoped their animosity would turn to something much different. His face went hot. "I didn't— I wasn't trying to—"

"Oh, I know." She waved a hand and laughed lightly. "I didn't think you were talking about *us*. That would be ridiculous."

Silas knew he should agree. He should laugh along with her about how absolutely incompatible they were, but he couldn't. Were they really that much different from Ron and Elise? They hadn't spent decades disliking each other. Sure, their past may be a lot more serious than a fight over electric cars, but there could still be hope for them. He wanted it to be true.

Maybe to make it true, he would have to do more than wish for a second chance. His heart pounded in his chest and his mouth went dry. Everything about the moment blazed in sharp relief. The corn in his hands, the certain slant of sunlight shining through the tree branches, the way her dark eyes watched him.

"I'm sorry for how I hurt you," he said. The words came out much softer than he'd wanted.

For a moment, he was afraid Violet would repeat the moment they had first faced each other in Fire and Brimstone.

"I know," she said.

"If I could go back and do everything differently, I would. It's my biggest regret."

"Thank you." There was a sheen of unshed tears in her eyes.

He wanted to say more. The time they'd spent together had changed him in a way that was hard to describe. She made him want to examine his darkest moments, even though he'd spent years avoiding taking more than a surface responsibility for his actions. Violet made him see the world differently. He looked down at the corn in his hands and prayed for the right words, but none came. Tossing the ear into the pot, he reached for another. He needed to be grateful for what he had— the opportunity to apologize. That's all he'd really wanted.

Well, that was all he had wanted when they'd first met. Things had changed.

"Thank you for the book. Again." She glanced at him.

"You've read it before, I'm sure."

She smiled. "Of course. I'm a huge fan of hers, but it's really neat to have an edition that old. Makes my heart go pitter pat to see it on the shelf." As if rethinking her words, she dropped her gaze and focused on the corn.

"Almost done out here?" Mrs. Tam asked from the back door.

"Last one," Violet said, holding up the ear in her hand.

"Good, then maybe Silas can come reach this pot for me." Mrs. Tam sighed. "Demetria put my favorite pot up high and I hate to disturb Ron and Elise. They look so cozy in the living room, all snuggled up—."

"Go, go," Violet said, laughing and pushing at Silas. "Quick, before we hear any more details."

"On my way." Silas was already on his feet. As he walked to the porch, he couldn't help smiling back at Violet, his heart lifting with gratitude. After everything he'd done, all the people he'd hurt and the trouble he'd caused, Silas never expected another chance with Violet. But grace had repaired one more relationship, in a way he hadn't even thought was possible.

CHAPTER THIRTEEN

"To sit in the shade on a fine day, and look upon verdure
is the most perfect refreshment."

— Jane Austen

"Elise isn't feeling well. I think I'm gonna take her home." Ron glanced back into the living room, his brow furrowed with worry.

Violet paused as she dried a dish pan and sneaked a look at Elise. She was sitting next to Silas on the couch, head back, eyes closed. Her face was pale. Silas was holding one of her hands, looking concerned.

"Of course, go right ahead." Violet's mom patted his arm. "I wore her out today. She's always got so much energy, I forget how old she is." She stopped as if realizing how her words sounded. "I mean, she's not much older than I am but—"

"She's a good twenty years older than you are, Shirley,

and she's five years younger than I am." Ron smoothed his beard. "I'm just worried about her. She's always had such spunk."

"It was too hot in this kitchen today." Her mother sighed. "I should have made her sit down more."

"I'm sure it's nothing," Ron said, but he didn't sound convinced. "I'll call you when I get her home."

A few minutes later, they were gone. Silas joined them in the kitchen. He was very quiet, his expression somber. Picking up a kitchen towel, he began drying the pots on the sink.

"She looked really pale, Mom. Maybe she should have a check-up." Violet put a casserole dish into the cabinet.

"Demi told her to take it easy today, but she just kept going. And she did have a doctor's appointment a few days ago. She's been feeling really tired."

They all worked in silence for a few moments. Violet glanced at Silas. "You and Elise seem close," she said.

"I broke into the Camden's house and stole all of her jewelry." His voice was flat. "They got back from visiting their kids in California for Christmas and found everything was gone, including her grandmother's wedding ring set and her father's gold pocket watch."

Violet realized her mouth was hanging open and closed it. "Did they get it all back?"

"Not everything. I hocked most of it in Twin Falls."

"She's forgiven you," Violet's mother said. "You shouldn't talk about that anymore."

Silas's expression hardened. "But maybe I should. It shows what kind of a person she is. She's welcomed me to church and sat next to me at the dinner table. She's treated me like a friend, when all I did was cause her heartache." He glanced at Violet. "I don't deserve her forgiveness, but she gave it anyway."

"True, she's a wonderful woman. But don't torture yourself over the past." Her mother cocked her head as a shrill tone sounded from the next room. "That's the phone. Ron couldn't have gotten to Elise's already, could he?" She left the dish in the soapy sink water and wiped her hands on a towel.

Violet felt frozen in place beside Silas, listening to the phone ring and her mother pick it up. She met his gaze and saw her own worry etched on his face. A faint murmur came from the living room and she didn't know whether to come closer or to stay put. After a minute or so, her mother returned but this time she had her keys in her hand.

"I'm so sorry to run out on you but Ron thought Elise looked too sick to leave her by herself. He brought her to the emergency room." Her mother's movements were jerky with panic.

"Mom, let me drive you." Violet started for the living

room.

"No, no. I'll be fine. We can't all rush over there. I'll go sit with Ron and let you know when they find out more." She waved on her way out the door. "Don't finish those dishes. Just leave them for me."

As the screen door slammed shut, Violet wrapped her arms around herself. She couldn't imagine the fear that Ron felt at that moment.

"Can I help you clean up?" Silas's voice cut through her thoughts.

"No, I can do it. You don't have to stay." She turned to him, feeling lost.

He hesitated, as if trying to find the right words. "I'd like to help, if you don't mind."

She considered telling him to leave but Violet wanted the company. Not just any company, either. If he had been any number of other friends or neighbors, Violet would have shooed him out so she could clean up without having to hide her fear and sadness. But Silas was different. He cared for Elise as much as she did, maybe more. He understood she wasn't going to be able to make happy small talk.

"Well, if you insist." She smiled, feeling strangely shy.

They worked in silence for a while, Thor watching quietly from the corner of the kitchen.

"I get the feeling he hasn't forgiven me yet," Silas said,

nodding at the dog.

"Hard to forget first impressions. Or so Mr. Darcy says."

He frowned at the plate he was drying. "So, you're a Pride and Prejudice fan?"

"Oh, not really. I probably butchered that line." Violet shrugged. "I read mysteries, mostly."

"Can I say I'm relieved?"

"Why, did you think I was going to start quoting whole scenes?"

"It just seems that so many women are looking for Mr. Darcy and I'm not Mr. Darcy." He didn't meet her eyes as he put a plate in the stack.

Her cheeks warmed. There were a few different ways she could interpret his words. He was worried about other women wanting Mr. Darcy and being disappointed with him…. or he was worried that *she* wanted Mr. Darcy and would be disappointed with him.

"What is that you don't like about him?"

"Oh, it's not that I don't like him. We're just different." Silas still hadn't looked at her.

"I don't know about that." Her heart was pounding. What was she doing?

"Because we're both jerks?"

"No!" She reached out a soapy hand, touching his arm,

desperate to make herself understood. "That's not what I meant at all."

"Okay. It's just that Luke said girls like Darcy because he's sort of a typical bad boy." He was looking at her hand where it rested on his arm.

"You know I've never liked the bad boy type. Otherwise, I would have chased after you when we were teens," she said, trying to lighten the tone of the conversation and failing miserably.

Bright blue eyes met her gaze. "I'm not sure if that's good news for me or not."

Violet thought about how she still hadn't moved her hand and how warm his skin felt under her fingers. Her mouth was dry. "Why— why is that?"

A corner of his mouth tugged up. "I'm a reformed bad boy. Can a guy ever really shuck off that label?" He seemed closer than before.

Her gaze dropped to his mouth. She could barely think straight. Silas wasn't the boy he used to be. That was one thing she knew for sure. "Yes."

"Definitely good news," he said softly.

He was just inches away. Everything faded into the background. The dripping faucet, the shrill sound of the phone, the pile of soapy dishes, the whir of the fan on the counter, even the overhead light reflecting on the kitchen window. She lifted her face to him, eyes falling closed. Again the phone rang but it sounded far away. Violet jerked backwards as it finally filtered into her consciousness. The *phone*!

"It might be about Elise." Her voice sounded high and breathy. She rushed from the kitchen without looking back.

She snatched up the receiver. "Hello?"

"What's going on? Why did it take you so long to answer?" Her mother sounded worried.

"Mom, I'm fine. Everything is fine here." She decided not to say she'd been ten feet away and not heard the phone. Her mother would never believe that. "How's Elise?"

There was a long sigh. "It's her heart, honey."

Violet tightened her grip on the receiver. "Heart?"

"She had an appointment last week and the doctor said there was a little arrhythmia and she needed to go to a cardiologist, but her heart just couldn't wait."

"How— how bad is it?"

"I'm not sure. They're still doing tests." Her mother sounded tired and sad.

"Can I bring you anything? How can I help?"

"Just pray, honey. I'll call you when we know more."

Violet said goodbye and slowly replaced the receiver. She turned to see Silas in the hallway, his eyes filled with worry.

"Her heart," Violet said and was embarrassed to feel

tears burn in her eyes. She didn't know Elise that well. Not like her mother did. But she'd always been around. Family barbecues, Sunday services, Christmas caroling in the winter, helping out with the summer reading program. "Still running tests." She could barely get the words out. "I'm sorry. You're closer to her than I am."

Silas wrapped his arms around her and for a moment, Violet forgot how complicated everything was between them. They were both hurting. She clung to him, letting herself give comfort and be comforted like two friends would. His heart beat was loud in her ear.

A low growl sounded behind Silas and Violet peaked around to see Thor in the kitchen doorway. His teeth weren't bared but his eyes were fixed on Silas.

"Uh oh," Silas said, letting her go. His eyes were red. "I don't think Thor forgives as easily as you do."

Violet couldn't help laughing a little.

"So, what can we do? Did your mom give you a list?" Silas still had a kitchen towel in one hand.

"She said to pray."

He nodded, and took her hand. "And then after that, we should call the prayer chain."

She stared at their linked hands for a moment and then smiled through her tears. She never could have predicted this day. An apology, a near kiss, a tender hug, and a prayer. All with Silas, the man she'd sworn to avoid.

Maybe it was time to imagine something greater than past hurts and awkward conversations. Maybe it was time to open her eyes to the possibilities right in front of her. As frightening as it was to let down her guard, Violet knew that mercy was calling to them both.

It was time to answer.

CHAPTER FOURTEEN

"If you will stay close to nature, to its simplicity, to the small things
hardly noticeable, those things can unexpectedly become great and
immeasurable."

— Rainer Maria Rilke

"Hey," Silas said softly. He didn't want to startle Ron as
he slept on the hospital waiting room couch.

The older man lifted his head, eyes half-open and
bleary with exhaustion, white hair sticking up on one side. He
sat up and rubbed his eyes before putting on his glasses. "What
time is it?"

"Four-thirty. I'm headed to Fire and Brimstone to put
in their new counter bar but wanted to stop by and see if there
was anything I could do." Silas sat down next to Ron. "Arcadia
Valley Community Hospital is one of the best in the state. I
know they'll take good care of her."

Ron nodded but didn't look encouraged. "The
echocardiogram showed blocked arteries. They're talking about
triple bypass surgery."

"When?"

"That's the problem. She's seventy-eight. And don't tell
her I told you or I'll be in the doghouse."

Silas wanted to smile but couldn't quite manage it. "I

don't understand."

He looked him in the eye. "Surgery has risks, and it's a lot riskier the older you get. Open heart surgery isn't having your gallbladder removed."

"Oh." Silas hadn't considered that the doctors would hesitate to help Elise. "So, what are they going to do? Because they have to do something. They can't just let her walk around with blocked arteries, can they?"

Ron shrugged, looking defeated. "They may just send her home with oxygen and put her on hospice."

Hospice. A shudder went through Silas at the word. Memories flashed in his mind faster than he could stop them. His mother being spoon fed. The hospital bed in the living room. The smell of antiseptic and the ragged sounds of labored breathing in the dark.

He patted Silas's hand. "Don't worry. They haven't made up their minds yet. There's still hope."

Silas nodded, suddenly feeling ashamed that Ron was comforting him instead of the other way around. "You didn't get much time together."

"That's true. But we understand each other, and that gives me a lot of peace about the situation."

In the quiet, Silas could hear the faint beep of machinery and the hum of the vending machines down the hall. "Violet said you two didn't always get along."

Ron smiled. "That's putting it mildly. We butted heads every time we met. Something about the way she approaches a problem just rubbed me the wrong way. I always wanted to correct her, tell her it's a lot easier to plow around the stump, you know?"

He didn't really, but Silas nodded again.

"One day your mom told me that Elise was sweet on me. And that was it." Ron snapped his fingers. "I was a goner."

"Sweet on you?" Silas was having trouble imagining how that would change everything so much.

"Well, words whispered in your ear are heard a lot better than ones that are yelled." He sat back as if it was clear.

"So, as soon as you knew she liked you, all your arguments stopped?"

"Oh, not at all. We're opposites. We still disagree." Ron snorted back a laugh. "It just changed the way I saw all the bickering we were doing. You see, when you love someone, things matter that don't usually matter."

Silas frowned down at his shoes. He'd always thought that love erased all difficulties, that when you loved someone you overlooked all their faults. He hadn't considered the idea of love making relationships more complicated. It made sense. Small slights from an acquaintance could be ignored, but would cut deep if they were given by someone you truly loved.

"When people get sick, a lot of times friends and family will rush to say all the things that they never took the time to say." Ron smoothed his beard. "But since Elise and I understand each other, I guess I feel like I need to tell you some things."

"Oh." Silas wasn't sure how to react.

"That girl you're dancing around? You need to just tell her straight. Tell her how you feel."

"It's more complicated than you can imagine."

"I doubt that. I've heard some pretty bad stories. I bet you did something to her way back when you were stealing and generally being a nuisance, and now you're trying to prove you're different."

"It's not like when I stole your ATV." He wished it had been. It would be so much easier to apologize for something that was simply a matter of money.

"Worse than when you hocked Elise's jewelry?"

Silas grimaced. "It's closer. It's just... I was mean to her, but in an everyday sort of way. She couldn't escape me and I knew it. The more it upset her, the harder I tried."

Ron closed his eyes for a moment. "You bullied the girl," he said softly.

"Every day for years." Silas felt his stomach roll with the familiar ache of regret.

"You don't think she'll ever forgive you?"

"I think... I think she has, actually. She takes that whole 'forgive your enemies' bit seriously." It was still hard to believe that not even twenty four hours had passed since his apology and her acceptance. "But she can't forget it."

"Of course not. Who could forget?"

Silas felt his heart sink. Somehow he thought Ron would have some special words of wisdom, something he could take and create a miracle for between them.

"But that doesn't mean she can't fall in love with the person you are now." Ron fixed him with a look. "Don't be so focused on what you did in your past that you force her to move on without you."

Hope flared inside him once more. *Move on without you.* She was moving on, it was clear. But was he going to stay behind, looking backwards at the kid he used to be? Or was he going to move forward and hope that Violet could see him as a person made new in Christ?

Violet unlocked Fire and Brimstone and shooed Thor inside. She'd been hoping that Silas would be waiting for her in the parking lot, but it was empty except for her own little four-door.

The restaurant was dark and silent. She wasn't an early

riser but this morning she was wide awake. She flicked the bank of lights and checked her watch. Maybe it was just worry over Elise, but her heart was beating faster than normal and she felt jittery. Her mother had returned from the hospital in the early hours of the morning and the news hadn't been good.

She thought of the moment when Silas had reached out for her and wondered if she was a terrible person for remembering it with happiness. Elise was seriously ill, and Violet was replaying how wonderful it had felt to be in Silas's arms.

Violet slumped onto a stool, not even bothering to try and focus on the book she'd brought to read while she waited. She was a mess. She'd been as steady as a rock for years, but for some reason she'd lost her bearings and was spinning around like a leaf in the wind. It really wasn't a mystery. Silas Black had that sort of effect on her.

A light tapping sounded at the door and she looked up to see him walking inside. She stood up, her heart in her throat. He was carrying a heavy leather tool belt, clearly ready for the installation of the counter bar. She could see his truck through the glass and noted a large trailer attached.

"Hey," she said.

"Hey," he answered, his eyes fixed on hers. Thor stood up behind Violet and Silas stopped a few feet away. "Hi, Thor."

The dog made a sound in his throat, as if he wanted to bark but knew he would get into trouble.

"No bloody noses today, buddy." Silas looked back at her. "And how's your... eye?" His cheeks went pink.

She laughed. "My eye and other parts are better. I never realized how hard our dining room chairs were before, I'll say that." She looked toward the door. "I thought you were bringing a helper. Unless they're in the trailer?"

He smiled. "Just the bar in the trailer. And my helpers should be here in about fifteen minutes. Jose Sandoz and Eric Cooper. Good guys. They work hard and are careful of the wood." He paused. "I stopped off at the hospital first to see Ron."

"How's he doing?" She shook her head. "That's a dumb question."

"I know what you meant. And he's doing okay, actually. He's at peace with the situation. Maybe because she knows he loves her. I think that helps a lot."

Violet's phone chirped and she checked the screen. "That was a reminder. I keep forgetting to print out the schedules for next week." She glanced around the dark restaurant. "Maybe I'll run do that while you wait for the guys."

"Sure." He nodded. "I'll hang out here. In the dark. Alone."

"Somehow I think you'll be okay."

His gaze fell on the book she'd left on the counter. "Already finished the Lehane?"

"No, this is just…" She waved one hand, as if that explained it all.

"Just?"

"Comfort reading. You know, those books you've read a hundred times and always turn to when you need a few minutes with an old friend." She laughed a little, as if she expected him to make fun of her.

He held out his hand and she placed the book in his palm. "Master and Commander? Great movie. Russel Crowe is amazing."

She snorted. "You're hilarious. I'm pretending you never said that."

"But seriously," he said, "it's a great book. This is your comfort reading? I didn't take you for a reader of nautical adventures."

"I love the whole series. The friendship between the doctor and the captain is my favorite part. Maybe because I've never had a friendship like that." She tried to speak matter-of-factly but there was a note of sadness, even to her own ears.

"Neither have I." He turned the book over in his hands. "But some books come close to it."

"Yes," she said, feeling the truth of his words slide into

her heart. "What are your comfort reads?"

He handed the book back to her. "I'm embarrassed to say."

"Oh, come on. It's not fair that you know one of mine and won't tell me yours. How bad can it be?"

"Someday I'll tell you. I promise. Just not today. It's—it's a long story."

She rolled her eyes at him but was more amused than angry. "Fine. Someday better be tomorrow. I'm going to go make those copies." Seconds later she was in the office and still smiling. Something had changed between them in the last few days. There was still awkwardness and a residual shyness that might never go away, but there was a new sense of trust. She didn't examine every word he said for a double meaning. He didn't seem to be afraid to talk to her like a friend.

Pulling the warm sheets from the machine, Violet stacked them on the desk and glanced into the little mirror above the desk. Her dark hair was growing longer and she wondered whether it made her look older or younger. Sometimes her students would tease that she didn't look much older than they did, and it was true. With her chin-length bob and small stature, she could pass for a middle schooler if someone didn't look too closely. Violet frowned at her reflection. Men didn't want to date someone who looked like a kid. Silas probably dated women who looked their age, with long legs and serious curves. He certainly wouldn't want to date someone a foot and a half shorter than he was. They must look ridiculous standing next to each other.

Letting out a grunt of irritation, Violet turned away from the mirror. She didn't care who Silas dated. It was none of her business and didn't affect her in the slightest. She repeated the words to herself as she left the office and headed down the long, dark hallway toward the restaurant.

A sound caught her attention and she froze, remembering the last time she'd rushed around the corner. Thor was barking, deep and loud. Angry voices sounded from the main area.

Violet crept forward, listening hard. Silas was speaking calmly, his words blurred together. Another man yelled an answer and Violet heard him clearly. "I said *get on the ground.*"

Her eyes went wide in the darkness. She didn't have to see to know his workers would never talk like that. *Jesus, help us!*

Silas spoke again, his words still unintelligible. Violet reached for her cell phone. Stepping backwards, she dialed 911. Whispering urgently, she gave the address and tried her best to answer questions. She wasn't even sure how many people there were. Sneaking forward again, she peeked around the corner.

Silas was standing near the front door. A bright circle of light from the hostess station illuminated the scene. He had his hands up and was standing in front of Thor, as if trying to shield the dog. A man in a dark shirt and ski mask pointed a gun at them both.

Violet stepped back into the hallway and told the operator it was just one man. "Please, please hurry," she whispered. She couldn't stand there and do nothing. Thor's frantic barking echoed through the restaurant. Peeking out again she saw Silas trying to reason with the man.

"I told you I'm alone. If you want me to get the cash, you have to let me go to the register." Silas looked calm but Violet could hear the careful tone in his voice.

"You think I'm stupid? The cash is kept in a safe in the office. Somebody knows the code and they're around here somewhere. They had to let you in. So, get on the ground with your dog and nobody gets hurt. And get him to stop barking!" The man stepped forward angrily and Thor responded with a lunge, growling deep in his throat.

Fear shot through Violet. Thor would never obey Silas. He might protect Silas, but he wasn't going to lay on the floor with him. *Lord, please keep them safe. Help me know what to do.*

"No, I'm telling you, she let me in and left. There's nobody else here and the money is still in the register, not the office. It's over there. And I have a lot of tools out in my trailer. Expensive tools. You can have those." A note of panic caught Violet's ear and she realized she was standing directly in the path of the robber. Silas was trying to lure him into another area, giving her a chance to leave the office.

"Then whose car is that outside?" The robber shouted at Silas, sounding more unhinged every moment.

"Who knows? It was here when I arrived," Silas said.

Her heart pounded as she weighed her options. She could hide somewhere in the office or even the bathroom next to it. Or she could head for the kitchen. The robber was hoping to find someone to open the safe, and that person would be her.

Stepping around the corner, she snuck toward the kitchen. Silas's gaze flicked toward her and then he got on his knees. "Fine, we can wait. You're right. She'll be back. She just stepped out for a second."

"You better call her." The robber reconsidered his words and said, "Give me your phone. I don't want you dialing 911."

Silas reluctantly handed over his phone. "She probably won't answer. She doesn't usually have it on her."

The robber stepped forward again and shouted, "I'm not stupid, so stop lying to me."

Thor barked and lunged, teeth bared. Silas looked from the dog to the robber, clearly trying to decide whether Thor could reach the man before he could squeeze off a shot. "Thor, it's okay, buddy." He didn't reach out to touch the mastiff. Thor wouldn't take well to either of them reaching for him at the moment.

Violet felt panic clawing at her throat and she willed herself to remain calm. If Silas called her, the phone he denied she was carrying would ring, and it was in her pocket at that moment. She was feet from the kitchen door but she fumbled for the phone, trying to turn off the ringer.

"Which one is she?" the robber asked.

There was a short silence and Silas said, "Romy."

"We're gonna do this on speaker so I'll know whether you lied to me," the man said.

Violet reached the kitchen and slipped inside, easing the metal swinging doors shut as quietly as possible. If Romy answered and Silas asked her when she was coming to Fire and Brimstone, she'd be confused. The man would know Silas had lied. Horrific scenarios appeared in Violet's imagination and she pushed them away. Violet could hear her own breaths in the quiet kitchen, sharp and fast. She looked around, praying for inspiration. There were plenty of knives but she wasn't sure she had the strength or the guts to stab someone. She'd also have to get very close. *Lord help me. I don't know what to do.*

She scanned the kitchen, whispering desperate prayers. She reached for a large sauté pan but then saw something better. Peels were neatly stacked on the counter and the long wooden handles seemed to beckon to her. Could she possibly get close enough without being seen?

Violet carefully lifted one from the stack and tiptoed back across the kitchen. Cracking the door, she listened hard. Romy's voice sounded in the restaurant, confusion layering her words.

"I don't understand. Why do you want me to get out of bed and come down there again?"

"Listen carefully—" Silas started to say.

There was the unmistakable sound of a phone being crunched under a boot. "I told you not to try and trick me!"

Violet felt sick at the fury in the robber's voice. Silas had done his best to buy her enough time to get out of the office but there was nothing more he could do. Sirens sounded faintly in the distance.

"Who called the police? Huh? It couldn't have been you." The robber was panicking now, backing toward the register. "She's here, isn't she? The girl who can get into the safe. They told me she'd be here."

Silas held his hands up, still on his knees. "She's not. Really."

The sirens grew louder but as relieved as Violet was to hear them, it only made the man more angry. He stalked back toward Silas and Thor, prompting the dog to let loose a series of deafening barks. The robber looked out the window at the red and blue flashing lights moving at speed toward the restaurant.

"You're a liar. I'm gonna go to jail anyway. Might as well get my revenge while I can." He wasn't shouting anymore. He was deadly calm.

Violet crept out the door of the kitchen, the handle of the peel gripped in both hands. She had never been the athletic type. Playing tennis in P.E. class had been the extent of her exposure to swinging anything heavier than a jump rope. She'd always been happy with her non-athletic body, more graceful than strong, fit enough for gardening and teaching but not dead lifting weights. Now Violet had never wished harder for six more inches and another forty pounds.

The robber stood over Silas, moving the gun between the dog and the prisoner. He was talking but Violet couldn't focus on his words over the pounding of her heart. The sirens were piercing now and the patrol car swung into the parking lot. Thor was barking non-stop. Silas looked up at Violet and gave the faintest nod, as if to say, "You got this." The robber lowered the gun at Silas and straightened his arm.

Violet swung the peel as hard as she could, closing her eyes at the very last moment.

CHAPTER FIFTEEN

"A morning-glory at my window satisfies me more than the
metaphysics of books."

— Walt Whitman

The shock of the impact knocked Violet off balance and she
stumbled to the left. Silas was on his feet in a flash, tackling the
man around the waist and slamming him to the ground. Thor
leaped forward and clamped his jaws around the man's leg.

The next moment police officers rushed into the
building, guns drawn, and Violet backed out of the way. Violet
knew better than to get in the way, but fear washed over her as
she saw the officers approach Thor and Silas, unsure of who
was the criminal and who was the victim. This was how
innocent people got shot, she thought, and for the first time
since the robber had entered the restaurant, Violet held her

breath in pure terror.

"On the ground, hands behind your head," an officer shouted.

Silas rolled off the robber and lay face down. Thor continued to growl and tug on the man's pants leg. The robber was fighting to get away, his ski mask was pulled up, completely exposing his face. Violet called to Thor and he lifted his head, confused by the shouting.

"Violet, can you call off your dog?" one officer asked.

It took her a moment to recognize Gloria Sinclair. All she had seen was the uniform and the gun. "He's really gentle. He's not usually like this," Violet said, then wondered why she felt the need to defend him. Of course Thor didn't usually use people as chew toys. She didn't usually get robbed, either.

Gloria nodded. "Just don't get in between them."

Speaking calmly, Violet put her hand on Thor's head and said, "Enough, Thor. That's enough."

He looked at her, his brown eyes ringed with white. Her heart squeezed at the thought of how much fear Thor had felt for her and for himself. Maybe not for Silas, but he certainly had seemed to understand they were on the same side. Thor let go of the robber's leg and stepped back.

"You're the one who called? Who are these guys?" The other officer moved forward, gun still drawn.

"I have no idea who that one is, but this is my friend

Silas." She reached out a hand to him, and he looked at the officer, waiting for permission.

"Sir, you can get up," Gloria said. "No injuries?"

Silas shook his head. "Not me, but he might have a bit of a headache later. She wacked him pretty hard."

The other office was cuffing the suspect, one knee in his back, but turned to smile in their direction. "We might have to deputize you."

Violet wanted to say something witty but the adrenaline that had carried her through the attack suddenly faded from her system and she sagged onto a stool. Thor nudged her leg and whined. Silas was beside her in a moment. "Are you okay?" he asked softly.

She gave a short laugh. "You were held at gunpoint, gave me time to get out of the office, tricked him into not calling my phone, and then tackled him... and you're asking if I'm okay?"

Looking back, she wasn't sure who reached out first. Holding each other tight, they stood there immobile for several minutes. Violet leaned back and gave Silas a tremulous smile. "You've got to stop letting me grab onto you when I'm upset."

"I was just going to say the same thing," he replied with a straight face.

They watched Gloria escort the man out to the patrol car and two more cars pulled into the parking lot. "Jose and

Eric are here," Silas said.

Gloria went to speak to them and the other officer cleared his throat, as if regretting having to interrupt their moment. "I'll need to get a statement from both of you."

Violet was glad that Silas was still holding her hand. She felt weak and sick to her stomach. "Everything happened so fast."

"I'm Officer Felipe Espinoza. I'll make this as quick as possible. I know you've had a shock. Did either of you recognize him?" He took out a notepad and a pen.

"No," Violet said.

Silas was quiet for a moment. "I think I know him," he said quietly.

She turned to him in shock. "How?"

"Just... around." He shook his head. "He used to hang out downtown. It was a long time ago, but I think it's the same guy. Justin-something. Kent, I think."

Officer Espinoza asked him more questions and Violet half-listened to the answers. There was no reason to be surprised that Silas knew the man. It was a small town. Really, it was no stranger than her knowing one of the officers that responded to the call. She tried to shake off a growing sense of unease. She needed to focus on the conversation. But as hard as she tried, the tender and fragile feeling that had been growing within her now withered under the bitter chill of suspicion.

Silas slid a glance toward Violet, his heart sinking at the flicker of emotion that crossed her face. He knew that look. It was the look of a person who was trying hard to believe something that didn't sound right. He gently released her hand.

"Sir?"

His attention snapped back to the officer. "Sorry. Say it again?"

Felipe said, "I know this it's hard to focus after something like this but if we wait too long, the details get fuzzy." Although professional, he was sympathetic to the feeling of shock. "Are you usually here this early, before the restaurant opens?"

"No, I was installing a counter today."

"Did he give any indication of having advance knowledge of the building or the occupants?"

Violet nodded slowly. "I heard him say that he knew I was here."

"You?" Felipe asked.

"Well, he said 'the girl who can open the safe'. I assume he meant me." She thought for a moment. "I think he said 'they told me she'd be here'."

Felipe frowned as he wrote in his notebook. "Certainly sounds like they knew people would be here alone. And who knows you've been coming this early to work on the construction?"

"A few people," Silas said. He looked worried. "I mean, it's no secret. But on the other hand, we don't come here every morning. It's random."

"Hm." Felipe made a sound that seemed to say that fact was significant.

"But if someone mentioned it in a crowded restaurant, it could have spread far and wide in hours." He could hear defensiveness in his own voice.

"I never mentioned it in the restaurant," Violet said quietly. She didn't look at him.

"Maybe your mother did."

"Maybe so." She was looking at Thor, a frown line between her brows.

Felipe looked from Silas to Violet. "If you could ask your mother who she told about the early morning construction, that would be helpful." Gloria came in the front door, leading Jose and Eric. He took out a card. "Call me if you remember anything more."

Violet took it and asked, "So, I'm not going to be charged for smacking him in the head?"

Gloria snorted. She clearly found the possible assault

charge a little less serious than Violet did. "You did a great job, Violet." She turned to Silas. "And you. I'm glad you didn't get hurt. This could have ended really badly."

Jose ran a hand through his hair. "Man, I want to say I'm glad I didn't get here early, but then I feel like I should have been here."

"No way. It was better this way." Silas put a hand on the young man's shoulder. "I wouldn't want to have to explain to your mom that you got held up at gunpoint."

"Do you guys want to take the day? Maybe start tomorrow?" Violet asked.

Silas looked at them and shrugged. "I'm okay to keep going. Wide awake now and everything."

They both laughed and even Violet smiled a little.

"But you don't have to stay." Silas wanted to reach out to her, but the expression he'd seen minutes before still haunted his thoughts.

She considered that for a moment. "I have to call my mom and let her know what happened and then I might go home. I want to make sure Thor gets somewhere he feels safe."

He watched her walk away and fought back the feeling that he had missed an important moment. He should have said something, done something, to make her understand. Her trust in him was wavering. Or maybe it had never been there at all.

Silas turned to Eric and Jose. "Excitement's over. Let's get started."

Eric headed toward the trailer, saying over his shoulder, "So, the girl took care of the robber? What were you doing the whole time?"

"Kneeling with my hands up," Silas said. He pointed to a spot near the stools. "And I don't feel an ounce of shame that she took him out and I didn't. I'm just glad she did."

Jose grunted. "A guy tried to break in one evening when I wasn't home and my wife dropped a nightstand on him from an upstairs window. They took him away in an ambulance."

"I never knew there was so much crime in Arcadia Valley." Silas had always thought he'd been the worst thing to hit the town, but maybe he'd been wrong.

"Nah, it's not too bad. I got my bike stolen when I was in high school, but I've never had any other trouble." Eric strapped on his tool belt and pulled on leather gloves.

Jose handed him a hammer and a box of nails. "I think it helps that we're kind of out of the way. Nobody comes through here unless they're planning to stay a while."

As they readied the equipment to transfer the counter bar to the restaurant, Silas thought about how easily everything could have gone wrong. He wasn't ready to go. Even though he'd apologized to Violet and she'd accepted, he had unfinished business. He wanted the peace that Ron spoke about earlier that morning. He didn't have the aching guilt that he'd had before their moment in the garden and he had some closure, but he needed more. His heart was aching from holding back all the words he wanted to say.

Eric and Jose carefully strapped a portion of the counter onto a rolling cart and headed for the front door of the restaurant. Silas stepped into the trailer to untie the next piece. The quiet darkness wrapped around him and he paused, closing his eyes for a moment. In his juvenile delinquent days he'd gotten in some sticky situations, sometimes even been afraid for his life. But this time had been different.

So many thoughts had flashed through his mind. Romy, Loki, Violet, his mother. A family of his own someday. He'd been afraid for Violet, and yet not afraid for himself. Not really. "He is my refuge and my fortress, my God, in whom I trust." He'd always read that Psalm as referring to physical safety, but it was more than that. His soul was secure in God, no matter what happened to his body.

And with that realization, he felt free. Silas looked out the trailer door at the sunrise and knew it was time to take a step forward. Not just in his work or his friendships, but a real leap of faith. As soon as he got a chance, he was going to ask Violet out on a date. He didn't want to die with any regrets.

"Don't worry, Mom. I'm okay. I promise." Violet had spent the last five minutes trying to calm her mother. She should have told her in person. Over the phone at such an early hour had been too much of a shock, but Violet hadn't wanted her to hear it from someone else.

"But you could have been hurt! Or worse…" She was crying again.

"I'm fine. So are Silas and Thor. We're all okay." The office seemed cold and ominous. Violet shivered and wished she'd brought a sweater.

"Tell me again what he said, the part about knowing you were there." She blew her nose into the receiver and Violet winced. Her mother shaken, but true to form, she was doing her best to get all the facts on what happened.

"I didn't really hear it all. He was talking to Silas."

"They're friends?"

"No. Maybe a long time ago." Violet got up from the office chair and sat next to Thor on the floor. She leaned over and rested her face on his neck. She didn't want to think anymore. She wanted to close her eyes and pretend none of the morning's events had ever happened. Maybe she could even go back to yesterday evening. She could pause everything right about the moment Silas had apologized to her, or maybe when he'd leaned in to kiss her.

There was a long pause. Her mother said, "Do you... Do you think— Maybe he's the one who—"

"No. I don't think so." Her voice was flat. "Mom, I have to go. I just wanted to let you know we're all okay. The police will be calling to talk to you."

"Maybe you should just close the place up for the day."

"But Silas is finished with the work he had to do in the shop. He needs to install it and get going on those butcher blocks in the kitchen." Violet couldn't imagine what the next week could hold. So much had changed just already.

"Well, he can put in the new counter but I'll rethink those chopping areas."

Violet wanted to argue but weariness overwhelmed her. It was unfair for her mother to cancel a word order because of some fragile connection between the armed robber and Silas. It was a small town. Everyone was a few degrees of separation from someone who had done something bad. "I'll let you know when I leave," she said.

After her mother had hung up, Violet lay there for several minutes, arms wrapped around Thor. He snuffed at her hair, giving her a tentative lick on the cheek.

"We have to get back out there, buddy." Violet didn't move. "We have work to do."

Thor gave her another questioning look and then stood

up, gently bumping Violet's head out of the way. She sighed and dragged herself to her feet. Her life in Arcadia Valley had been comfortably boring until Silas returned. Now it seemed that every day was more tumultuous than the last. She'd loved her peaceful life, her predictable routine. Any kind of emotional upset or drama and she'd run in the other direction. Then why did she feel as if being separated from Silas would break her heart?

As she left the office, Thor by her side, Violet thought of how much she'd worried over the possibility of puppies a few days ago. If only she'd known, a litter accidental puppies was going to be the least of her worries.

CHAPTER SIXTEEN

"Mistakes are always forgivable, if one has
the courage to admit them." —Bruce Lee

Silas put the phone down and stared at the dashboard of his truck. Loki snuffled into his shoulder, her giant mastiff head bumping his arm repeatedly.

"Yeah, I'm going." Silas turned the key and felt the powerful engine roar to life. Mrs. Tam had been polite and diplomatic but she hadn't pulled any punches. Since the robbery investigation was still ongoing, she felt it was best if they postponed the butcher block project until the police found the link between the robber and his inside knowledge.

Putting the truck into gear, Silas slowly pulled out of the driveway of his shop and turned onto the highway. His first thoughts hadn't been for a lost commission, but of Violet. He hadn't seen her since the robbery, but assumed they'd meet again at the restaurant. Did she suspect him, too? He had no real reason to drop by her house or for her to come to his. He had no way of knowing what was going on in her head.

He drove downtown, barely noticing the buildings he passed or the other cars on the road. Officer Felipe had taken his statement and said he'd call if he needed anything else. Maybe there'd been some new development, something that implicated Silas. Of course he hadn't been involved but circumstantial evidence with a shady past, and things could look pretty bad.

"All I can do is pray," he said out loud. Loki lifted her head and huffed at him. "What else do you want me to do?" he asked. "I can't exactly go over there and plead my case. Maybe she doesn't feel the same way as her mom, but maybe she does."

As if sensing the irritation in Silas's voice, Loki gave him a chastened look.

"I know, you're in a bad position, too." He reached out and rubbed her behind the ears. Loki was definitely acting differently than a few weeks ago. Silas wasn't a betting man, but if he had been, he'd say puppies were on the way. "Maybe for your sake, I better make sure you and Thor don't end up separated for good."

The sky was perfectly clear and the sun was beating down, but what had started out as a perfectly beautiful summer morning in Arcadia Valley had turned gray and colorless to

Silas. All the optimism he'd felt as he'd rolled out of bed was gone. Just as he'd started to think that Violet might feel something more than friendship, it had evaporated into uncertainty again.

Friendship. He winced at the thought. They had never been friends, and that was most of the problem. There was no trust to balance out the suspicion. All he could do was wait and pray for the best.

Jenny Johnson adjusted the microphone at the lectern and looked out at the congregation. "For Elise Camden, who remains in the hospital. Lord, hear our prayer."

"Lord, hear our prayer," Violet responded with the other parishioners. There still hadn't been any decision on Elise's medical treatment. Ron was sitting a few pews ahead of her, Silas next to him. The men had their heads bowed and Ron's shoulders were slumped, as if he carried the weight of the world.

Her mother leaned over and whispered, "We should visit her after church."

Violet nodded but wondered whether Silas would be there. They hadn't spoken more than a few words since the robbery. She could say it was because of her schedule and how hard they'd both been working, but that wouldn't have been true. After her mother had canceled the butcher block cutting areas, Violet hadn't known whether to contact Silas or not. She'd hoped that he would call her, or maybe even come by, but she hadn't heard anything from him since. After the trauma of the robbery, she felt like his silence was another layer of pain over an already horrible episode.

She snuck another look at Silas, wondering what he was thinking and if he had even considered calling her. Then she tried to shake the thought from her head. There was already so much to do, she didn't need to be obsessing over Silas. The restaurant was short-staffed again. Bernadette hadn't even lasted the week. She had to interview more applicants and train another waitress.

Even as Violet reprimanded herself for thinking of him, her gaze traveled back toward Silas. Her emotions were in a constant state of flux. One moment she was sure that the man had changed and there was something real between them. The next she was revisiting the moment the robber had insisted that Violet was in the restaurant. The police still had no real leads on the accomplices and Justin wasn't talking. If only she knew for sure, she might be able to reach out to Silas herself.

As they stood to sing another hymn, Violet realized that she missed one thing from the days when they were teenagers. She'd always been able to tell when he was lying. To Violet, he had always been an open book. Teachers had believed his stories and excuses, but Violet had seen right through him.

But now everything had changed. She wanted to think she could tell when he was being untruthful, but her emotions were overshadowing her better judgement. When he smiled at her, she forgot what she was saying. When he leaned close, she didn't even remember to breathe. Her perspective was gone. The old Violet would have been able to tell whether Silas had been involved in the robbery, but the new Violet couldn't concentrate on anything other than how he made her feel. She had never felt so vulnerable.

"Lord, make me an instrument of your peace," they sang. She needed peace. She needed perspective. "Where there is hatred, let me sow love; where there is injury, pardon..." Violet had always been a peacemaker, the type of teacher who brought students together. It had been effortless. "...where there is doubt, faith; where there is despair, hope; where there is darkness, light; where there is sadness, joy." Her life had been easy before Silas had come back to town. She was above all of the gossip and fighting, even among her friends.

"O, Divine Master, grant that I may not so much seek to be consoled as to console..." Violet had sung the words a hundred times before. She'd known the song since before she could read. She found herself hearing them in a new way. When Silas had first tried to apologize, she'd refused him. Of course it would have given him peace. She hadn't wanted that. She'd wanted him to suffer. "…to be understood as to understand; to be loved as to love…" Anytime Silas had seemed like he was offering an olive branch, she'd rebuffed him.

"For it is in giving that we receive…" Tears burned in her eyes as Violet struggled to sing the words. She'd allowed Silas to say he was sorry but she'd made him work for it. She'd thought she was giving him the gift of her forgiveness, but it was Silas who had given her a gift by reaching out, again and again.

"…it is in pardoning that we are pardoned." Violet saw herself clearly for the first time in years. She'd been carrying around a grudge and the only person it had been wounding was herself. Silas's apology hadn't freed her from all the pain of his bullying and teasing. That would never come until she put down her burden and reconciled herself with the past. "And it is in dying that we are born again to eternal life."

As the song ended, Silas slid the hymnal into the pocket of the pew and glanced back at her. Their eyes met and he smiled tentatively. Violet dropped her gaze, hoping her tears hadn't been obvious from where he stood.

For years Violet had hoped Silas was suffering the

consequences of his actions, paying for all the hurt he'd caused. Even after they'd grown closer, a small part of her wanted him to feel the humiliation and fear she'd felt.

How wrong she'd been. Silas had made peace with God, and as best he could, with her. He had moved on. She was the one still stuck in the past.

And the only person who could make it better was herself. Regardless of the details on the robbery, Violet still had work to do.

Violet hovered at the doorway to Elise's hospital room. The beeping of the machines and the antiseptic smell had her on edge. She hadn't been in a hospital since she'd broken her arm at age twelve.

Peering inside, she could see Luke, Romy and Mrs. Delis were already in the room. Elise was being treated for a heart ailment and Violet wondered if she might not appreciate seven visitors at a time. "Maybe we should come back later. How about an hour from now?" she asked.

"You just come on in," Ron said, waving them inside. Silas stood and offered Mrs. Delis his seat. She smiled at him but shook her head. Silas looked at Violet, gesturing to the chair and she debated for a moment whether to accept. If she didn't, they would all be standing with two empty chairs, which was silly. If she did, she would have to cross the room and come closer to Silas. Just as a shadow of sadness passed over his face, she decided. She would have to take the first step, literally, to bridge the gap between them.

"Thank you," she said and settled into the chair next to Elise's bed. Romy smiled at her from where she stood next to Luke. They were close, but not touching. If it didn't blossom into something more, Violet would be very surprised. Reaching over, Violet took the older woman's hand. "Can I get you anything?"

"A new heart would be grand," Elise said, smiling.

There was an uncomfortable pause and then Ron laughed. "That's my girl. Never loses her sense of humor."

"So there's no decision yet?" Violet's mother reached out to Elise on the other side of the bed.

She shook her head. "Still waiting. And I hate that I left you in the lurch for the canning. You're probably so far behind."

"Don't you worry for a second. Not one." Mrs. Delis managed to sound fierce and loving at the same time, her thick Greek accent softening the tone of her voice.

Elise smiled. "That wasn't an answer."

"Everything is under control. Whatever you need, you know you can count on us." Violet squeezed her fingers gently.

"I don't have to be back in the classroom until late August. We have plenty of time to get everything done."

"Except the tomatoes are all harvested and getting them processed into sauce is a big undertaking." Tears shimmered in Elise's eyes. "I just hate letting down my friends."

"Oh, hey." Ron leaned in and kissed her forehead. "You're not lettin' anybody down. No way."

"We're almost done. Few more days." Mrs. Delis looked at Luke and Romy. "Summer is a big feast here. Always was. Always is."

"Right," Luke said. "I'm helping Romy put up their produce, too. Stavros is coming home to help out for a few days, Nico and Charlotte were pitching in yesterday, and Theo is back from his camping trip to the Sawtooths. It's harvest time and we're all working hard. But when haven't we had to prepare and can around our schedules? It's always this way."

Silas added, "We're doing fine, but of course we miss you."

"You've always been so good to me. All of you." She looked around at them. "Every time I need help, someone is already there, taking care of it. Silas is watering my garden and Demi took some canned food to the library to pay my fines." She noticed Violet's confused expression. "Charlotte, the director, started Food for Fines. You can pay off your fines with a donation for the food bank."

"You've always been the one helping out when there was a need," Luke said. "Now it's our turn. Don't worry. Everything is okay."

Romy hadn't spoken yet and Violet noticed her eyes were shining with tears. Of course being in the hospital room must remind her of when her mother passed away. Violet glanced at Silas and noted the tenseness in his jaw and the straight line of his mouth. He was struggling, too, and not just because Elise was ill.

"Now, you all go out and have a great afternoon. You don't want to spend all your time in here with me," Elise said.

Violet started to protest at the same time as Silas. "We don't mind—"

"Of course we want to stay—"

Elise held up a hand. "I'm real grateful for your visit but what a waste of a sunny day for you all to stay in here." She looked from Silas to Violet. "Go take those dogs out for a walk. Maybe they'll hit it off."

Luke snorted. "I'd say they already hit it off too well."

"What does that mean?" Mrs. Delis asked.

"They got friendly with each other when Violet brought Thor over to help with the garden." Romy shrugged. "Nobody was watching."

Ron started to laugh. "Oh, boy. I didn't see that one

coming."

Elise looked confused for a moment before a smile bloomed on her face. "Well, that's wonderful!"

"Nothing is for certain," Violet said. "It would be better if it was just a false alarm."

"Well..." Silas frowned up at the ceiling.

Violet shot him a look of surprise. Was he going to say he wanted them to be raising puppies together? They had enough trouble just having a conversation that didn't devolve into tears or apologies.

"Loki's been acting oddly," he said.

"Uh oh," Violet said. "How oddly?"

"You can't tell yet, can you?" Violet's mother asked.

"It's only been a few weeks but there are signs. She's got a few chew toys she likes. She'll drag them around and hide them under the table, things like that. But now, it's just weird... She's sort of adopted one and sleeps with it, like it's a baby." Silas shook his head. "Maybe it's nothing."

"Nope, sounds like she's feeling broody." Ron hitched his thumbs in his belt loops. "Congratulations, you two. I mean, you four."

"It's not really a good thing." Violet tried to temper the irritation in her voice. "We've got potential vet bills, appointments, and finding homes for the puppies, just to start."

Elise wasn't deterred. It was as if she'd been told Christmas was coming early. "If it's the money, I can help out," she said excitedly. "We need a litter of beautiful mastiffs in Arcadia Valley. How exciting!"

"No, no, we'll be fine," Violet said quickly. It wasn't really about the money. It was just so awkward to think of them being connected that way. She glanced at Silas and saw the same hesitation on his face. It wasn't planned, but here they were, doing the best they could with what was given them. Of course puppies were wonderful. Everybody loved puppies. But it seemed to happen out of the blue. She wasn't prepared. She hadn't even considered it. If she had, she would have seriously thought on whether to go through this with Silas, the man she used to hate but now... Now her feelings were so different, so much deeper. She was afraid to even put a name to them.

"I'll be praying for puppies," her mother said, looking happier than Violet had seen her for quite a while. She was fairly bouncing on her toes. "You'll have to start planning on where her birthing place will be. It has to somewhere she feels safe, but also gives her some privacy. I bet Silas could make a beautiful whelping box."

Violet started to say Silas had better things to do than building whelping boxes in his spare time but he was nodding. "I'm sure there are some good plans online. I'll look around."

"It's going to be a lot of work. I'm sorry that most of it will land with you guys." She looked to Romy.

"We'll all pitch in," Romy said. She smiled for the first time. "To be honest, I can't wait. If it turn out she isn't having puppies, I'm going to be very disappointed."

"Well, whatever happens, is God's will," Mrs. Delis said.

"Of course it is." Violet felt like a Grinch for being so hesitant about the puppies. "I just wish we'd had more warning. Or maybe even some choice in the matter."

"Well, timing has a lot to do with the outcome of a rain dance," Violet's mother said. She looked positively giddy.

"Mom, I don't know what that means."

"It's just a saying," Elise said. "Something us old folks like to spout when we want to sound wise. It means we're usually the ones behind whatever is happening to us."

Violet started to protest. "But we really had no intention of—"

"Now, you kids get outside and enjoy the sun. I can't stand thinking of you wasting such a nice day in here with me." She lay back on the pillow.

As much as they insisted they wanted to stay, Elise was having none of it. She accepted a hug and kiss from each, then waved them away. "Go," she said. "Go and do something exciting for me. I'm stuck in here but you don't have to be.

Use those strong hearts and muscles. Go for a swim, take a hike, run around with those dogs. I'll rest up here, and I'll be smiling when I think of you young people out there having a good time." She looked paler than she had just a few minutes ago.

As they silently made their way down the hallway, Violet thought of Elise's words. *Go and do something exciting for me.* She wasn't the adventuring type. She really enjoyed her quiet life, working in her garden, teaching her eighth graders, helping out her mom, playing with Thor. She wasn't the kind to rush out and jump off a cliff. But Elise's directive touched something deep inside her. She only had a little time on this planet, and if she wasn't going to use it wisely, what was she doing here?

"Hey, what do you guys think about taking a hike?"

"Sure," Silas answered. "We can bring Thor and Loki. They'd love it." He paused, looking at the others. "I mean, if everybody is free."

Luke shook his head. "I'm on call and I can't get too far from the hospital."

"Romy?" Violet asked, feeling a sudden flash of panic. *Please, say yes.*

She shook her head. "I'm sorry. I can't. Charlotte's coming back to help me organize the basement pantry and check that the jars are all sealed."

"Do you need help? I can lend a hand, too," Luke said. "I just might have to run to the hospital if I get called."

Romy's cheeks went pink but she sounded perfectly normal. "Sure. That would be great."

"Oh, I forgot about the canning." Silas grimaced.

She put a hand on her brother's arm. "Don't worry about it. You've worked hard all week and I appreciate everything you've done already. You guys go ahead. Like Elise said, it's sad to waste such a beautiful day being inside."

Violet swallowed hard. Her mother hadn't acted any differently toward Silas in the hospital room, but the fact she'd postponed the new project seemed to hang over them all. She couldn't trust her emotions and there wasn't any resolution about the robbery, but she was going to have to decide, one way or the other how she and Silas moved forward.

Silas seemed to read the doubts in her eyes and said, "Maybe it's not the right day for a hike. It's pretty hot outside. We could just stay home and read where it's cool." He caught himself and hurried on. "Separately, I mean. Different books. In different places."

Violet watched his face turn a dark shade of pink and tried not to smile. It was rare that Silas expressed anything less than perfect confidence. "Hm. Maybe. If I do, I'll be reading Master and Commander. And you?"

She could see him debating whether to respond but

then he decided to give her the answer he'd withheld the day of the robbery. "Probably The Secret of the Caves or The Clue in the Embers."

Violet's mouth dropped open in surprise. So, the unflappable bad boy Silas Black loved the Hardy Boys. She couldn't have predicted that in a hundred years. "The Mark on the Door is good, too."

"One of my favorites."

Luke and Romy were watching them with puzzled expressions. "So, are you guys not going? That's a shame," Luke said.

Violet cleared her throat. Her pulse was pounding as she came to a decision. She was going to take her elderly friend's wisdom to heart in a way she hadn't anticipated. Spending the afternoon with Silas, far away from any distractions of the city, wasn't what she'd envisioned when she'd made the invitation, but her life never seemed to go as planned around her old nemesis.

"I'm still up for a hike."

His eyebrows rose. "Well, I guess it's just the two of us."

"Guess so," she said, trying to sound nonchalant and feeling as if she were failing miserably.

"Great," Romy said. "Now I don't have to feel guilty for ruining your afternoon."

Luke flashed them both a smile and opened the door for Romy. As they all filed out into the blazing summer morning sun, Violet tried not to smile. She really shouldn't be surprised that something so simple as a group hiking invitation had turned into a cozy and intimate outing. It seemed that no matter how Violet tried to keep Silas at arm's length, they ended up back in each other's orbits, like planets pulled together by forces beyond their control.

Sneaking a glance at him, Violet noted the set of his mouth and the hunch to his shoulders. She didn't know if it was good or bad that Silas felt as uncomfortable as she did at the prospect of spending the afternoon alone.

CHAPTER SEVENTEEN

"Nature's first green is gold,

Her hardest hue to hold."

—Robert Frost

Silas tried not to think of how awkward it was going to get in the next few hours. Violet didn't seem to be as suspicious of him as her mother, but she definitely had doubts or she would have dropped by or called. Clearly she thought there was some possibility he'd been involved in the robbery that threatened both of their lives.

As they walked into the parking lot, Silas tried giving Luke a distress signal but either his friend was unconcerned, or he was oblivious to Silas's subtle hints. Silas figured it was the latter when Luke and Romy drove off minutes later. They said goodbye, but Silas felt like they were abandoning him without a backward glance. Of course he didn't fault Luke for taking any opportunity to be close to Romy. Silas had to admit he was a little bit jealous of the way they seemed to be moving so easily from friendship to something more.

"Where are you parked?" Violet asked.

"Eastern corner," he said, pointing.

"Me, too."

He fell into step beside her, trying to think of something entertaining to say. The heat shimmered off the blacktop and Violet brushed a hand across her forehead. Silas thought of someplace cool and quiet to go. Maybe the park at the end of Main, or take a dip in the swimming hole. No, not the swimming hole. A memory flashed into his mind and he almost groaned out loud. The summer between seventh and eighth grade he'd gone there with friends. Violet and two girls were already there, splashing around the deep pool under the rope swing. Five minutes of shouted teasing and the girls had scrambled out. They'd glared as they gathered their towels and marched away, but Silas and his friends had simply laughed. Mission accomplished, they'd gotten the swimming hole to themselves.

Silas slowed as he saw that she'd parked a few spots away from his truck. "So..." he said, wishing he had some of

Luke's natural glibness. He bet when Luke asked Romy out, it hadn't been in a sweltering hospital parking lot surrounded by dirty cars.

"You really don't have to hang out with me. I just thought of it because Elise and somehow it sounded like a good idea." She wasn't looking directly at him, but rather focusing somewhere over his left shoulder.

"I know," he said, laughing a little. "I don't mind. Honestly."

"Don't mind," she repeated. "That's not exactly the same as wanting to spend the afternoon with someone. How about we don't, and say we did."

He knew she was trying to be funny but he didn't laugh. He was gripped with the fear that she was going to get in her car and drive away without understanding what he'd been trying to say. He'd once quoted Same Spade from the Maltese Falcon to her but he wasn't a tough guy from the mean streets. He just a carpenter who was trying to say what was in his heart. "I said 'don't mind' but actually should have said 'really, really want to'."

One brow went up and she hesitated, as if trying to decide whether he was serious. "I guess it could be a doggy play date."

"Not that they need any encouragement on that front."

Her lips twitched. "True." A moment later, she

sobered. "So, what do you want to do? Walk around Arcadia Creek Park?"

Silas looked up at the bright blue sky and prayed for inspiration. *Lord, help us get past this place, past what I've done.* But there was nowhere in Arcadia Valley that didn't have some connection to that time in their lives, however fragile the link. From that realization, another idea took shape but he would be taking a leap of faith just suggesting it.

The heat seemed to kick up a notch and Silas felt a bead of sweat slide down his back. Waving her toward the shade of a tree at the edge of the parking lot, he waited until they were out of the glaring sun before asking, "What about taking a drive?"

"Drive? Like down country roads?"

"Like… out of this town." He stopped there, watching her for the fear and suspicion that surely would flicker in her eyes.

To his surprise, she started to smile. "You have a destination in mind? Or are we just hitting the highway with two giant mastiffs and driving until we have to stop?"

"I was thinking about hiking the canyon, but just heading off into the wilds doesn't sound bad at all. Road tripping with Loki and Thor could be a thing."

"Loki, Thor and seven puppies," she corrected. "Even better."

"We'd have to get a motorhome."

She was laughing out loud as she swept her hand across an imaginary window. "I can just see the stickers on the back. Girl person, boy person, big dog, big dog, little dog, little dog, little dog, little dog, little dog…"

"My mom always got a kick out of Juan and Julia Gonzalez's car window stickers. They have the four kids, two cats, and their dog. Takes up most of the window." It was a bittersweet memory. His mother had always wanted a large family. She hadn't made any secret of her miscarriages, but she didn't speak about it very often. It made her too sad.

As if sensing his change in mood, Violet's laughter faded away. "She really loved the school kids."

"She loved all kids. She really was looking forward to having grandkids someday."

"Oh," Violet said softly.

"She died without any regrets and she was secure in her faith, but I see Romy with Luke and I wonder what it's going to be like for her when she starts a family. At least Mrs. Delis is there to be a grandma." He shook his head. "If Romy does get married and have kids with Luke, I mean."

She smiled. "It's hard not to jump to that when you see them together, right?"

"Pretty obvious, isn't it?" It didn't bother him as much as it had just a few weeks ago. Maybe he was getting used to the idea.

"Yeah, it is." She seemed wistful, looking up at the leaves of the tree above them. "They seem really happy. There's nothing better than friends who fall in love, don't you think?"

"Agreed. Although I've never been in love," he amended.

"Me, either. I hadn't even really thought much about it until..." Her cheeks turned pink. "It's probably just the age, you know? Everybody starts falling in love and getting married and having kids." She looked around the parking lot. "So, what were you thinking?"

"About marriage? Or kids?" Surprise made him stutter but he wanted to be honest with her. "I wasn't really thinking about it. I mean, I have. More recently than before I moved back to Arcadia Valley. And maybe you're right. Maybe it's just the age when people start getting married and it seems to pop up everywhere." He felt like he wasn't explaining himself very well. "Not all the time, but more than before. It just seems more of a possibility now when a few years ago I never would have wondered what kind of dad I'd be or noticed how long some people have been married."

She was looking at him, as if trying to puzzle out his reasoning. He hurried on. "The Camdens were married fifty five years. That always seemed impossible to me. But I can see it now. If you make a vow before God, it means something."

Violet nodded. "I know what you mean."

"Sometimes I'm worried that I won't be a good husband because I never saw a marriage up close like that. After my dad died, my mom just didn't seem interested in remarrying. But she was a great mother and I hope I can be a good parent like she was. Maybe it doesn't matter and striving to be a perfect parent is an impossible dream. Maybe we all just bumble along as best we can and we pray God fills in the gaps," he said.

Violet bit her lip and seemed to be choosing her words carefully. "I think you'll be a great dad," she said softly. "And a great husband."

Relief rushed through him.

"But before… when I asked what you thought, I was asking about our plans for our hike," she said.

His relief turned as quickly to intense mortification. "Oh, right." He wanted to rewind the last few minutes, right up to the point he thought she'd been asking about his existential angst and not his afternoon plans.

"Thank you for sharing that, though" she said quickly. "I feel the same way. It all seems so scary to me. How do people stand up there and blithely take a vow that will last their entire lives? How do they take home a tiny infant whose life is literally in their hands?" She looked up at the leaves again. "I just don't know if I'm that brave. I love reading all those mysteries and thrillers, with fierce people doing outrageous things, but I'm really pretty weak."

"I don't think you're weak at all." He'd tried his best to break her and she'd survived. Not only survived, but emerged stronger than ever. And then she'd forgiven him. He couldn't think of anything stronger than that.

He started to speak but the shrill ring of his cell phone interrupted his sentence. "Sorry," he said as he took it out of his pocket. Glancing at the screen, he frowned. "Ron's calling."

Fear passed over Violet's face. They had just been there in the room with Ron and Elise. "Maybe he forgot to tell me something," he said, his chest tightening.

Putting the phone to his ear, he could hardly hear his greeting over the beating of his heart. "Everything okay?"

"They can't wait any longer." Ron's voice was thick with emotion. "I had to make a decision."

Silas swallowed hard. "We'll be right back. We're still in the parking lot."

"No hurry," Ron said. "No reason to hurry now."

He froze, the phone to his ear. He needed to know what had happened, but couldn't get the words out. Violet stepped forward and took his hand, her eyes filled with tears.

Ron cleared his throat. "They say the surgery will take three or four hours. I just wanted to let you know that she took a turn and we had to make a choice. I hope I did the right thing. She was okay with just going home but I convinced her to push for the surgery. I just can't let her go yet. I know I said I could, but I can't."

Silas almost slumped with relief. He closed his eyes, regaining his composure. He had been so sure that they would be planning Elise's funeral. And they still might be. Bypass surgery at her age was risky at best.

Violet squeezed his hand and he looked down at her, forgetting that she couldn't hear the whole conversation. "Thanks for letting us know. We're coming back up there."

Ron said goodbye and Silas slipped the phone back into his pocket. "They took her into surgery," he said.

Her eyes went wide and he could see her readjusting her emotions. "Oh. I thought…"

"I did, too." He looked down at their linked hands and thought of that shining moment where they'd been planning their afternoon together. He'd imagined letting the dogs play at Centennial Waterfront Park while they spent some time alone, just the four of them. Just as quickly as disappointment flooded his emotions, it faded away. He and Violet were just where they were meant to be.

Her love and loyalty to her mother had brought Violet to the restaurant for the weeks he'd been working there. His love for Elise and Ron had thrown them together again. Her friendship with Romy had united them in the garden. Over and over, they had ended up side by side because of their love for their friends and family.

He looked into Violet's dark eyes and felt more sure of her than he had of almost anything in the last few years. People said timing was everything, and Silas wished he knew whether he should speak now, or wait until the end of the day. It wasn't a matter of whether he would declare himself to her, but when. Violet had walked into his life and changed everything around, reminding him of who he wanted to be and how far he had come.

She squeezed his hand. "We'd better head back inside," she said softly.

Silas nodded and together they stepped out of the shade of the tree, and toward the long hours ahead. Ron had told him not to waste time and Elise had told him to seize the day, but Silas knew that sitting vigil with a friend was where he was meant to be. If he was given a chance, God willing, he would tell her what was on his heart, but for now, Elise and Ron came first.

Violet tried to calm her heart as they walked back toward the hospital. What she had been hoping and wondering over had finally come to pass. Well, perhaps not completely and definitively, but she was holding Silas's hand. *Silas*, the guy whose name had made her stomach clench for the past decade. Silas, the person she'd talked to God about for years, trying not to hate him because she knew hating someone was wrong, but at the same time, unable to be stronger than her feelings. She glanced up at him, in awe at how their lives had come together in the last few weeks. Jamie might think she'd lost her mind, but what had happened between this former bad boy delinquent and the girl he had bullied wasn't crazy. It was miraculous.

CHAPTER EIGHTEEN

"And Spring herself, when she woke at dawn,

Would scarcely know that we were gone."

— Sara Teasdale, Flame and Shadow

Jamie handed the iced mocha to Violet and sat down on the hard plastic chair beside her. Her cheeks were flushed from the heat outside but Violet knew her friend would regret wearing shorts and a light T-shirt if she spent any amount of time at the hospital. The place must have top-notch air conditioning because Violet was freezing, even with the sweater she'd brought from the car.

"Any news?" Jamie asked.

"Nothing yet." She glanced at the swinging doors at the end of the hallway. Ron, Silas, and Mrs. Delis were in the waiting room just to the right. They were solemn but calm, praying every so often, joining hands and entreating God to guide Elise's doctor's hand. Violet had never realized what torture a waiting room could be for families who waited for news, and she couldn't imagine what it would be like to keep that vigil alone.

"I saw your mom when I was getting the mochas," Jamie said, pausing to take a sip. "She said when she went to pick up some keys from the restaurant, the police came by to talk to her."

Violet sat up. "Why? Was there another break in?" Fire and Brimstone was closed on Sunday. The police would have called unless it was important enough to track down her mother in person.

She shook her head, her blond hair brushing her shoulders. "They finally got the guy to talk. Justin whatever-his-name was."

"Kent," Violet said. Silas had been right about the last name.

"Yeah, since it was an attempted armed robbery, he decided to trade information for a plea deal."

Violet grimaced. She wanted to know who had given him information, but the article in the paper said he'd lived in Arcadia Valley a long time ago, just returning from Boise. Plagued with a drug addiction, the guy had a long rap sheet of trespassing, shoplifting, assault, battery, and burglary. Somehow, he always seemed to spend the minimum amount of time in jail. Violet shivered at the memory of their encounter. The man had been desperate and shaking with anger.

"So, how did he know I'd be there?"

"Remember that waitress who only showed up for a day or two? I can't remember her name. She had red hair and lots of make-up," Jamie said. "I guess she was scoping the place out for him."

"Bernadette," Violet said. Bernadette had practically begged to handle the deposits and paperwork, even though she'd been hired for waitressing. "That makes so much sense now."

"I wonder how she knew your mom needed help. Probably saw a flyer at the Gas N Shop." Jamie leaned back in the seat, trying to get comfortable. Her mocha was half gone, a layer of water visible from the melted ice.

"No, I remember she said that Silas told her..." Violet felt the words die in her throat. Bernadette had said that Silas had told her about the job and that they were friends. Silas had known Justin, too. The one connection between the robber and his accomplice was the man sitting right down the hallway, the one her heart had grown to love.

Jamie gave her a puzzled look. "Well, it doesn't matter now. The police arrested her this morning. She'd been hiding at a friend's place in Twin Falls, but people talk. It wasn't hard to find her, I guess."

She nodded, trying to focus on the conversation. The condensation made the plastic cup feel slick in her hands and Violet set it on her knees, shivering at the touch. Or maybe it was from the fear that was racing through her. Silas had always been able to fool the gullible people around him. Violet had always been able to see through him. Until she couldn't.

Doubt bore down on her with a crushing weight. The more she thought about it, the more she realized that with Silas, there was no even ground. It was high or low, emotions running hot or cold. Maybe she was one of those women who was addicted to drama. Maybe she had subconsciously sought out a relationship with Silas, knowing he would cause her pain and grief.

"Are you okay?" Jamie asked, putting a hand on her shoulder.

"I'm fine. Just... thinking." She closed her eyes for a moment. She couldn't make her mind stop grabbing at details, flashes of memory. Everything Silas had said or done now seemed ominous. All of his time at Fire and Brimstone had been innocent-looking enough and the beautiful redwood counter bar that he'd installed was the shining jewel of the seating area, but he'd made a point to get a good look at other areas of the restaurant. He'd known more than most about the way the place worked, and he didn't even have to pry, like Bernadette. Violet had told him everything he needed to know.

She felt her chest tighten and tried to take deep breaths. She'd been such a fool. All those moments of emotional connection, when she'd felt God moving them together were overshadowed with double meanings. Picking tomatoes in his garden like a regular guy, going to the same church service as she did, befriending Elise and Ron as if he actually liked old people, giving her the Dorothy L. Sayers book, doing dishes at her mom's house— it all seemed different now. His heartfelt apology had clearly been just one more step in his plan. He'd been a con artist as a teen, and he hadn't changed.

"I need to go... run an errand." She stood up, unable to stay there and face her foolishness any longer. "Can you tell them I'll be back later?"

Jamie stood up, concern in her eyes. "Are you sure? Why don't we tell them together and I can come with you?"

"No, I'm sorry. I have to hurry." Violet was already walking away. She had to be alone. She had to think without Silas's good looks and clever words distracting her. Her mind had to rule over her heart, because clearly her heart couldn't be trusted.

Silas looked up as Jamie came into the room and knew immediately that something was wrong. Her pretty blue eyes were troubled and as she greeted them, her smile was tight.

"Violet had to run an errand." She shifted her feet, as if

unsure whether to sit down.

Mrs. Delis patted the chair next to her. "Come here. Tell us some news so we don't worry so much."

Ron nodded. "I turned off the TV. What a load of junk. And that laugh track was giving me a headache."

"Well, the police told Mrs. Tam that they found the person who gave them information about Fire and Brimstone," Jamie said.

"Great news. I was afraid they'd never catch the guy." Ron hesitated. "Not that I doubted Gloria and Felipe and the chief. It's just hard to track down these criminals sometimes, especially when they won't talk."

"It was one of the servers," Jamie said. She was looking at Silas. He thought over the servers he knew and couldn't imagine any of them being part of a robbery. "Her name was Bernadette," she said.

"A shame," Mrs. Delis said, shaking her head. "Who can you trust?"

Jamie dropped her gaze and Silas felt several key pieces of information slide together. He knew Bernadette. She was friends with Eric Cooper, the guy he hired to help install his larger jobs. She'd brought Eric lunch a few times. When she'd said she was looking for a job, Silas had let her know that Fire and Brimstone was short-staffed. And now Violet had disappeared, sending Jamie to tell them the news in her place.

She thought he was the same criminal he had been so many years ago.

"Can I get anybody anything? I can run to the store or…" Jamie bit her lip.

"No, honey, we're all okay. Thank you," Mrs. Delis stood up and gave her a hug. Jamie relaxed into it, her face still tense with anxiety but her body returning the comforting embrace. "You're a good girl," Mrs. Delis said, leaning back and patting her cheek.

Her cheeks went pink. "Thanks, Mrs. Delis. And I better get home. I've been at the restaurant a lot and my dad needs help sorting the buckets for the season."

Ron perked up. "The blueberries are almost ready?"

"A few more days. Maybe a week. He just likes to sort out the broken buckets before we start so it's not a rush to buy some more. The weather's been perfect so we think it's going to be a bumper crop, especially the Rekas and the Olympias."

"Somethin' to look forward to," Ron said. "Elise loves fresh blueberries. She won't be picking her own this year but I'll make sure she gets enough to freeze up for the winter."

Despite his own turmoil, Silas felt a stab of sadness for Ron. The unspoken worry wasn't that Elise wouldn't be well enough to pick the blueberries, but that she wouldn't be around to enjoy them at all.

After Jamie left, Silas stood up. "I need to walk for a

while. I'll just be outside, getting some air. Call me if you hear anything."

"Of course." Mrs. Delis patted Ron's arm. "Shirley will back soon. We'll take care of Ron for you."

He nodded and tried to smile. Mrs. Tam had been polite enough earlier but that certainly would have changed. When he reached the hallway, Silas fought with despair. He felt the hope of the last few weeks slip through his fingers, and a crushing sense of doom take its place. Violet thought he was involved. He remembered the look she'd given him when he'd told the officer that he'd met Justin before. Mrs. Tam had told him to hold off on the butcher block projects despite any other evidence of his connection, so this would only add fuel to the fire of her suspicion.

Silas stepped into the elevator, pushing the button for the ground floor without really seeing. If only he could hold on to the last few moments he'd had with Violet. The press of her hand in his, the love in her gaze, the softness in her voice. She had trusted him and seen him as a friend— more than a friend. When they'd almost kissed in the kitchen, he'd known she felt the same way about him and despite the chaos of the last week, he'd taken that shining moment and held it close as proof. But as always, life had a way of throwing him a curve, and although he should have seen it coming, it still took him by surprise.

CHAPTER NINETEEN

"Thousands of tired, nerve-shaken, over-civilized people are beginning to find out that going to the mountains is going home; that wildness is a necessity"

— John Muir

Violet stood under the tree near her car, arms wrapped around herself, tears sliding down her cheeks. She needed to think, needed to look at all the evidence logically, but she'd spent the last ten minutes fighting back the agony of betrayal.

Gathering her thoughts, she looked at the branches reaching up into the blue sky. There wasn't anyone to go to for advice. Her mother didn't know their history together. Jamie knew, but didn't seem to truly understand how traumatic it was. She wasn't that close to Romy, and if she had been, she wouldn't have felt comfortable enough telling her about falling for Silas. Elise was too sick. Ron was too worried for Elise. Mrs. Delis was comforting and supportive, but she had a no-nonsense attitude that made Violet wonder if she'd just advise her to move on.

Wiping her cheeks, she thought of how hard she'd tried to move on, move forward. In church the verse of the hymn had been like God speaking directly into her heart. *Lord, make me an instrument of Your peace.* But did that mean giving Silas the benefit of the doubt, or just forgiving him for what he'd done? *Where there is hatred, let me sow love; where there is injury, pardon.* Their hatred had turned to love, at least for her. She was so afraid that it had been all in her imagination and Silas felt nothing for her. *Where there is doubt, faith; where there is despair, hope.* Violet closed her eyes and offered up all her doubt. She didn't lack faith in God, but she couldn't find her footing with Silas. It seemed that despite all the good he did, the ways he took care of the people around him, his gentleness and love for his friends, Violet just couldn't stop doubting him. Every time hope grew between them, the tiniest voice of doubt would cast her into despair.

Where there is darkness, light; where there is sadness, joy. She needed God to shine a light on the situation. She wanted to bring joy out of sadness, but she just couldn't do it alone. Her wounded past kept her from being that person. Maybe if she simply opened her heart and gave God permission to do whatever it was He needed to do… Violet straightened her shoulders. That was it. She'd stop trying to force the issue one way or the other. She would simply offer herself as God's instrument. Humility had never been her strong suit but she was at the end of her ability to discern the situation. She knew what her heart wanted, but she didn't know what God wanted.

"Violet?"

Ironic. She'd just been asking for humility, and she'd gotten her first dose. There was nothing like letting out a shriek and jumping when someone called your name.

"I'm sorry. I didn't mean to scare you." Silas was already backing away, hands up.

"No, it was all me. I didn't hear you."

He nodded but stayed where he was, at the very edge of the shade. Stuffing his hands in his pockets, he said, "I heard about Bernadette."

"I should have figured it out. She was asking a lot of questions."

He met her gaze and glanced away. Violet tried not to see that as an expression of guilt but her heart was pounding.

"I know her. Sort of. She's friends with Eric, a guy I hire every now and then."

"She mentioned that she knew you." Violet wanted to step forward and say something reassuring but stayed where she was.

"I'm sure it looks suspicious."

There was no use in denying that it did. She'd been standing out in the sweltering parking lot, crying in the shade of a tree because it had nearly convinced her that Silas wasn't anything like the person he pretended to be.

"Would it help if I said I had nothing to do with it?"

"Yes," she said, but her voice wasn't very strong.

"But it wouldn't convince you. Not really." His shoulders were slumped as if he carried a heavy weight.

She started to shake her head. *Where there is doubt, faith.* In the next moment, Violet felt her suspicion fade away and a rock-hard assurance took its place. Not even two hours ago they had stood in this spot and she'd said how hard it was to imagine getting married. She couldn't see how two people took vows that would last for a lifetime. It had seemed impossible. Now she understood. It was a gift, a grace that allowed two people to step out in faith. But in order to receive it, she had to open her hands and humbly trust.

"It does." She smiled at him. "It makes a difference."

"Are you— are you sure?"

"Yes," she said, laughing now. "I am. I had a little…" She waved her hands, trying to find the word for what she'd been doing under the tree. "Crisis of faith."

"In God?"

"In you." She gave him an apologetic glance. "All of this time I've been watching for signs that you were lying and were up to no good. I was half-convinced I'd find out the real truth any day now. I worried and examined everything you said and did."

He grimaced. "I'm so far from perfect. My pride gets in the way and I—"

She stepped closer to him and took his hands. "That was wrong of me. Maybe in the very beginning, it was right to be suspicious, but after we'd become friends, it was wrong to keep watching for some sign that you were lying." She dropped her gaze, shame burning her cheeks. "You hurt Elise and Ron but they accepted that you'd changed. Everybody did but me. I thought I was giving you a chance, but deep inside, I still looked for evidence. I think I almost wanted you to be guilty so I could be right in not trusting you." It was hard to admit that part to herself, and even harder to say it out loud.

"Violet, I have to tell you something. I should have said it sooner but…"

"Elise got sick, and then we got robbed, and now she's in surgery? I know." Violet smiled. "But you can tell me now."

Silas wished that they were somewhere nicer, maybe walking along the canyon like he'd wanted. They could be looking out at the emerald green river, Thor and Loki beside them. Instead, they were sweating under a tree at the hospital, surrounded by blacktop and cars. But if this was his opportunity, he was going to take it. "If I could have chosen who I was going to fall for, there would have been thirty other girls on the list before you."

The corners of her mouth slowly pulled up. "Is that so? Not a very romantic thought."

"Sometimes the truth isn't really pretty." He watched the smile spread to her eyes. Violet understood. They weren't going to be like Luke and Romy, or Nico and Charlotte. They weren't about tender first dates and sweet moments. They were complicated and busy and always running to help someone else. There would be time for candlelight dinners, but for now, the moment of truth was just as it was supposed to be.

Silas stepped closer. They were the most unlikely couple in the history of Arcadia Valley... Except that they were also just right for each other. Falling for Violet had brought him peace and forgiveness in a way he could never have predicted. "If I'd known you were in my future, God would have had to drag me to Arcadia Valley, kicking and screaming," he said.

"He didn't?"

"I came here willingly because I had no idea. Not even a glimmer."

She laughed. "Not even a hint?"

His gaze dropped to her mouth. He wanted to hear everything she had to say but his heart was more interested in kissing her. "Did you?"

"Oh, yes." Her eyes were half closed. "If I'm honest with myself, there was one moment when I knew I was going to fall for you."

When she didn't say anything more, Silas pressed the softest of kisses against her lips. She kissed him back, warm and soft.

After a few moments, he drew back "You know I have to ask."

"When I saw you reading the Maltese Falcon." Her voice was breathy. "Nobody reads those old classic mysteries but me. Or so I thought. And when you quoted it…"

He lifted his head. "But that was way back—"

"The first day we met. I didn't say I was happy about it. In fact, I was determined to stay out of your way. But of course, that didn't work out. God had other plans for us."

Silas pulled her close and whispered in her ear. He said all the things he'd wanted to say for so long, but hadn't had the courage. As Violet clung to him, he realized that grace and mercy had always been waiting for him, no matter what the circumstances. All he'd had to do was reach out, arms wide open, and let it in.

Violet stood on tiptoes again and he lowered his head to press a kiss to her lips. He'd never get over the wonder of her, of all people, being there in his arms.

"I love you, Silas Black" she whispered.

His heart ached in response, his happiness almost as painful as grief. "I love you, too."

He kissed the top of her hair and thought of how love had arrived exactly when needed, without pretense or fanfare. After he'd apologized and she'd accepted it, a tenderness had grown between them. That tenderness had blossomed in the soil of his forgiveness. It had grown strong, rooted in their friendship, and had finally born fruit.

That fruit was love, one of God's greatest mysteries.

Epilogue

"In times of joy, all of us wished we possessed a tail we could wag."

— W.H. Auden

Violet watched as her mother and their friends filed into the room. Silas slipped his arm around her and they stood together like proud parents. Thor lay beside them, his nose pressed through the slats of the pen, touching Loki's neck.

"Oh, aren't they darling?" Mrs. Tam breathed, hands clasped together.

"Just remember they'll grow up to be Thor-sized. That's a lot of dog when you're already running a full-time business." Violet didn't want to discourage her mother but she couldn't imagine a mastiff running around Fire and Brimstone.

"You understand what family get-togethers are going to be like now?" Stavros asked, peering into the large crate of wriggling puppies. Loki woofed softly and gazed back at her visitors.

"Always the logical one," Luke said, clapping his brother on the back. "Come on, live a little."

"And that's exactly what I don't tell the kids," Stavros said, rolling his eyes. "And like Violet said, they're going to be huge."

Nico came to stand beside them. "Huge and the best friend you'll ever have besides me. It's not even up for discussion for me." He shot a glance at the beautiful blonde next to him. "I'm blaming this on Charlotte."

"And I'll blame it on Elena," she said, pointing at the little dark-haired girl beside her.

Elena beamed. "Papa said it was a surprise. I didn't even know I could ask for one."

"I think it was Luke's idea that we keep them all in the

family," Romy said, trying to be helpful.

Violet laughed as all the brothers turned toward Luke. "Yeah, definitely Luke's fault," said Theo. He had just moved back to Arcadia Valley and was going to teach seventh grade. Jamie had nagged Violet until she got as many pertinent details as she could. Not that she blamed Jamie at all. If she wasn't already in love with Silas, she would be giving them a second glance. As it was, she barely noticed the overload of good-looking men in the room.

"I think we should get that one, there." Elise pointed out a brindle colored puppy asleep on its side. Its brothers and sisters were busy eating and her chosen puppy was napping. "It seems to be about our speed," she said.

Ron gave her a kiss on the cheek. "Anything for my future bride." Elise was still recovering from her bypass but as soon as she'd left the hospital, they'd started to plan their wedding. "He can be your service dog."

"More like my exercise coach," she said. "Taking it for a walk will be good for me." She put a hand to her forehead. "And now I think I should sit down."

As Nico and Ron rushed to find her a chair, Violet glanced at her mother. "I didn't mean to be negative. I think you'd do great."

Her mother smiled at her. "Oh, I know. But you're right. I'll just enjoy all the puppies around. I have enough on my plate."

"Me, too," sighed Mrs. Delis. "With the garden and café and Elena, I don't think I could manage another thing."

Charlotte cleared her throat and looked at Silas, a question in her eyes. He nodded. "Well," she said, "Elena has something to say about that."

"Now?" The little girl bounced on her toes. "Do I get to tell them now?"

"Go ahead. You've been a great secret keeper for the past week." Charlotte smoothed Elena's ponytail.

"Papa and Charlotte set a date for the wedding," she cried out.

The resulting exclamations and good wishes and hugging made Thor sit up and let out several large barks. The puppies were startled from their dinner and started to let out tiny yips of confusion. Violet looked at Silas and couldn't help laughing. She never could have predicted the joy in that moment. Not the puppies, not the crowd of friends, not the sweet announcement. It had all been a surprise from start to finish. From the first day Silas had shown up in Arcadia Valley, her life had changed for the better.

Silas leaned down and whispered in her ear, "Good. Between Ron and Elise, and Nico and Charlotte, they'll be exhausted from all the planning. We'll be free to plan our wedding with as little interference as possible."

Our wedding. Violet's heart caught in her throat and her eyes filled with tears. She hadn't thought the moment could have gotten better, but it had.

As they stepped forward to congratulate Nico, Charlotte and Elena, she had the feeling of moving forward in more than one way. She had spent years being afraid of what was ahead, being cautious and wary. That time was past. Her wounds had healed and her scars, though visible, weren't painful to the touch. Life opened up before her, full of mystery and excitement. She wasn't afraid any more. She was stepping out in faith, Silas by her side and her heart filled with hope for the future.

THE END

Dear reader,

Thank you for reading Summer's Glory, the second book in my new series set in the fictional town of Arcadia Valley, Idaho. I hope you enjoyed reading it as much as I enjoyed writing it!

The idea for Violet and Silas came to me after hearing about a case of bullying in our local school system and the community's response to it. Bullying is nothing new and it affects thousands of students a year, but awareness is helping head off the kind of experience Violet endured. During the conversation about bullying in my community, many people shared their own experiences with bullying, some even explained how they still felt pain decades after they had left high school. I started to wonder— what happens when years pass and the bully/bullied children grow up? How do people overcome the guilt of having acted so badly, and the pain of being emotionally abused long term? And once forgiveness happens, is it ever possible for a real friendship or love to bloom? I believe that it can, but only through the hard work and determination by the people involved, and the grace of God.

Violet never shared her pain with her mother because she didn't want to add to her mother's worries. A lot of children hide their experience from their parents, and this only makes the bullying worse, as parents continue to push for activities and relationships that put the bullied child in harm's way. One of the best ways to head off bullying is to make sure children feel safe to share the negative things that could be happening in their social circle. Violet still had difficulty sharing her struggles with her mother, even as an adult. She learns through her new friendships that it's okay to ask for help, and that being vulnerable doesn't mean she's weak.

Silas was a troubled kid, no doubt about it. He's angry, mean, and a thief. When he harasses Violet, day in and day out, he's trying to find the power and stability that's missing in his own life. Silas continues to hurt others until he's finally held accountable for his actions, and then his heart begins to change. It takes a lot of courage to face the past and accept responsibility. Silas also has to believe he's forgiven, and be able to make amends with a clear conscience.

When Silas and Violet first meet again, years after high school, she refuses to believe he could change into anything better than the bully he was. Silas wants to make amends, but he still believes— deep down— that no one will ever trust him again. They both must learn to let go of the past, and see each other for the person they are now.

I hope this story helps someone let go of hurts that happened many years ago, or perhaps helps someone else embrace the possibility of forgiveness. Approaching someone we've hurt and asking for forgiveness is a true act of courage, and I pray that your apology is received with an open heart!

Love,

Mary Jane

Recipes

Violet's Very Bestest Pizza Dough

Violet and Silas spend a lot of time at Fire and Brimstone although we don't get to see them in the kitchen during the story. Of course, when they've resolved their differences and are completely content with each other, they're going to spend a lot of time in the kitchen together. After Silas builds Violet a brick oven for her backyard, Friday night make-your-own pizzas with friends become a weekly tradition. But you can't make a really great fire-grilled pizza without a great crust, so this is Violet's Very Bestest Pizza Dough. Enjoy!

Ingredients

1 cup warm water (105°F to 115°F)

1 envelope active dry yeast (2 ¼ tsp yeast)

2 1/4 cups (or more) all purpose flour (whole wheat flour works wonderfully, too)

1 1/4 teaspoon sugar

1 teaspoon salt

4 tablespoons olive oil

Instructions

Dump the yeast into the cup of warm water and let sit for five minutes until the yeast is puffy and happy. Yeast party!

Stir the flour, sugar and salt together. Make a little well in the center and pour in the yeast/ water mix with the olive oil. Begin to mix gently until fully incorporated. It will be sticky and a bit of a mess.

Bring it to a floured cutting board and knead it, adding a few teaspoons of flour to keep it from sticking to your hands. You may have to add flour as you go. This is an important step and if you don't know how to knead dough, you can look it up on Youtube. It's very easy. Fold it in half and push forward away from you, flip ninety degrees and repeat for about five minutes. The dough should be nice and stretchy when you're done.

A lot of people have good luck getting their dough to rise in a dry bowl but I always wipe mine down with a little oil. It keeps the dough from sticking and it rises faster. So, place it in the oiled bowl and cover with plastic wrap or a damp towel. Place in a warm spot and let it rise for about an hour. If you have quick acting yeast, it may not take that long. While it's rising, go read a book or play with the cat. (But don't go clean the house. That's definitely not in the recipe.) The time spent waiting for your pizza dough to rise is worth it, I promise.

When it's doubled in size, punch it down (free anger therapy!) and lay it on a floured surface to begin rolling it out.

Don't be afraid if air is trapped at the edges. That will make for some really fluffy and crispy edges. It can be stored in an airtight container in the refrigerator for a day or two, or frozen for a little longer. Pizza dough is not a soufflé. It's pretty durable.

Fire and Brimstone's Famous Kimchi Pizza

I'd always avoided kimchi because I'm not a fan of cabbage, but a trip to Seattle convinced me that kimchi can be delicious! It also helps if you find a variety that isn't burn-your-face-off spicy. (I'm not a fan of that, either.)

Once you've had kimchi on pizza, you'll crave it. Maybe not every week, but you will. It's one of those unique flavors that just can't be substituted by any other pickled vegetable or topping. This recipe uses the most basic ingredients, but delivers a fantastic but subtle blend of Korean flavors.

Ingredients:

One cup of kimchi in your favorite variety

If you've never tried it before, I recommend picking out several small jars for a taste test. I prefer a mixed vegetable variety, but my husband likes the cabbage only version best. It also comes in several heat levels so read the labels carefully. It's no fun if your taste buds are fried before you get the chance to taste the food. (My personal opinion. Others in my family disagree.) It's also very easy to make at home so if you like pickling, consider trying a few jars of your own home grown kimchi.

2 tbs rice vinegar

2 cloves chopped or minced garlic (okay, you can get away with one, but I love garlic, so for me it's two minimum)

1 tsp oil (sesame, if you have it)

¼ cup kochujang

This is a red pepper paste that's in most grocery stores. It's related to the pepper that Mrs. Tam puts in her famous sauce (see below). Now, a spicy kimchi and a full ¼ cup of kochujang is a little much for me, so I keep the sauce a little spicy and tone down the heat level of the kimchi. But hey, if you're brave enough, dial that back up and see what you think. My husband makes his own kimchi pizza for good reason. He says my version isn't even "warm". (I think he's just killed his tastebuds.)

Mix all ingredients together and spread on the pizza to the edges. Sometimes I add some green onions or scallions if they're around. My daughter likes to put fresh spinach on hers, and another adds pineapple for a spicy-sweet combo.

Sprinkle with mozzarella cheese and bake at 500F for about 15 minutes. Enjoy!

Mrs. Tam's Fresh-From-The Garden-Super-Secret Pizza Sauce

Now you all know this is based on fictional characters because I would never reveal a super secret recipe. It's against the girlfriend's guide to keeping your friends (especially friends who cook delicious food).

Not only does this spicy sweet pizza sauce go with anything and everything, it freezes well for several months. We like to freeze ours in ziplock bags so we can defrost them easily in a pan of warm water. Instant homemade pizza sauce!

Ingredients:

6 ripe tomatoes

3 TBS olive oil

2 cloves garlic

2 tablespoons fresh basil

1 teaspoon salt

½ tsp sugar

½ tsp black pepper

1 tsp dried oregano

2 teaspoons fresh parsley

2 tsp gochugaru or other red pepper flakes

In a small sauce pan, blend the olive oil, garlic, dried oregano, red pepper flakes, pepper and salt. Stir for about five minutes on medium-low heat until very fragrant. Don't let it burn! If it starts to clump together, add a small bit of water and lower the heat.

In a blender or food processor, add six chopped, fresh tomatoes, fresh parsley, basil, sugar, and the heated spice paste. Blend until smooth but don't over blend. You can add a little more salt or pepper to taste, if needed. This thick and chunky sauce is the perfect base for pizza toppings or dipping for breadsticks. Enjoy!

OTHER TITLES by Mary Jane Hathaway

Austen Takes the South Series

Pride, Prejudice and Cheese Grits

Emma, Mr. Knightley and Chili-Slaw Dogs

Persuasion, Captain Wentworth and Cracklin' Cornbread

Leaving Liberty

Cane River Romance Series

The Pepper in the Gumbo   Book One

These Sheltering Walls   Book Two

Only Through Love   Book Three

A Star to Steer By   Book Four

The Boundless Deep   Book Five

Until Winter Comes Again   Book Six

To Look On Tempests   Book Seven (Spring 2017)

Arcadia Valley Romance Series

Romance Grows in Arcadia Valley   (Boxed Collection of Six Inspirational Novellas)

Summer's Glory (Arcadia Book One)

OTHER TITLES by Virginia Carmichael

Colors of Faith Series (historical Christian romance)

All The Blue of Heaven

Purple Like the West

Denver Homeless Mission Series

Season of Joy

Season of Hope

A Home for her Family

BIOGRAPHY

Mary Jane Hathaway is an award-nominated writer of Christian fiction and a home schooling mom of six young children who rarely wear shoes. She holds degrees in Linguistics and Religious Studies from the University of Oregon and lives with her habanero-eating husband, Crusberto, who is her polar opposite in all things except faith. They've learned to speak in short-hand code and look forward to the day they can actually finish a sentence. In the meantime, she thanks God for the laughter and abundance of hugs that fill her day as she plots her next book. She also writes under the pen name of Virginia Carmichael. You can find her on her facebook author pages of Mary Jane Hathaway or Virginia Carmichael, on the cooking blog Yankee Belle Café, on her personal blog The Things That Last, or at Huffington Post where she blogs about all things books.

Now for a sneak peek at the next book in the Arcadia Valley Romance Series!

Muffins and Moonbeams

by Elizabeth Maddrey

Then Jesus declared, "I am the bread of life. Whoever comes to me will never go hungry, and whoever believes in me will never be thirsty."
John 16:35

Malachi Baxter pushed a hand through his hair and scowled at the computer screen. He hadn't built a website since high school. How did he get stuck with this job? Oh, right. Business degree. Which meant handling the finances and such, but the website? He scooted away from the machine and stood. He needed to talk to his brothers.

He stepped out of the tiny office at the back of the bakery and into a wall of heat. His oldest brother, Jonah, was measuring ingredients into a huge mixing bowl. His lips were moving, but with his brother's face half-turned Malachi couldn't quite lip read well enough to make out the words. Was he singing? He touched Jonah's shoulder.

"Hey, Mal. Done with the website already?" Jonah set the measuring cup aside and dusted his hands on the apron tied around his waist. "That was fast."

Malachi shook his head and signed. "We need to hire someone. It's an investment that'll pay off in the long run. If I do it, it's going to look like someone's ten year old put it together over the weekend."

Jonah laughed. "That bad?"

Malachi nodded. He'd drag his brothers back to see what he'd been playing with all morning if they insisted, but it was embarrassing.

"All right. Let's check with Micah, but if you say we need it and can afford it, then I'm game." Jonah strode across the kitchen to the swinging door that led to the front of the bakery where Micah manned the counter.

Malachi sighed and followed.

Micah handed change and a bag of bread to one of their regulars—Malachi searched his memory for the name and came up blank—and turned when the light above the door that served as the hearing impaired version of a door bell flashed and the customer left. "Uh oh. If Mal's out of the office, something must be up."

Malachi clutched his stomach and feigned laughter before sticking his tongue out.

Jonah shook his head. "Nothing serious. Mal thinks we should hire the website out."

"Rusty?" Micah raised his eyebrows.

Malachi signed, not bothering to speak along with it since they were alone in the bakery. "When was the last time you did a website?"

"Fair enough. Works for me. You notice I didn't volunteer to do any of that stuff, right?" Micah squatted and collected a towel from under the counter. He ran the cloth over the display case, scrubbing at some imagined spot. "Do what you think is best."

Jonah nodded. "Agreed. And since you're handling all the business end, I don't really care about details. You've got a good head on your shoulders and won't dig us into debt."

It was good his brothers had faith in him. Someone needed to. He nodded and eased back through the door into the kitchen. No point in hanging around out where customers came to gawk at the deaf man. In D.C. he hadn't been a novelty. There were all sorts of people in the greater metropolitan area that made up what had been home his whole life. And mostly people didn't bother staring at the ones who were different. In Arcadia Valley different stuck out. Oh, they were nice about it. Malachi doubted anyone genuinely had any motive other than learning about something they didn't encounter every day. But that didn't keep him from feeling like a circus sideshow because he couldn't hear.

Back in the office, he pushed the door mostly shut, a signal that he was involved and shouldn't be disturbed if at all possible. A quick search online revealed what he suspected, there were more web designers in the world than made sense.

How did he sort out the bad ones and find the good? Malachi drummed his fingers on the desk and reached for his cell phone to tap out a quick text to his sister, Ruth. The B&B had a nice site with a lot of the same kinds of functionality that they'd need. He set his cell back in the cradle and turned to the computer. It was mid-morning. Ruth was probably cleaning rooms and wouldn't get to her phone for a while. But there was no rush.

With a glance toward the door and only the barest twinge of guilt, Malachi started up Orion's Quest and logged in. There weren't many players online in the middle of the morning, but there were always folks in other time zones, or people, like him, sneaking in a battle during a slow time at work. He skimmed the activity log. No one he played with was on, but he'd been storing up solo missions. Maybe he could knock one of them out. If his ship was repaired. He'd parked it in a dry dock when he logged out the night before, there should have been enough time for the fixes to be finished. And if not, he'd wander this outpost—where was he again? Didn't matter, really. Some new outpost on the edge of civilized space, getting ready to head into the frontier and see where his fortune lay.

Before that, he could use an armor upgrade. Maybe some new weapons. If he had the cash after he paid for repairs.
The chat bar at the bottom of his screen notified him that Scarlet Fire had logged in. His heart sped up and he grinned as he opened up a direct message box.

"What are you doing on in the middle of the morning? Don't you have work?"

"Ha ha. I could ask you the same thing. Slow day?"

Malachi glanced at his cell phone cradle before typing again. "Waiting on a text. Thought I'd check on my ship, maybe start a quest."

"Need a first mate?"

Colorful lights flashed in the corner of his eye. Of course. He sighed and grabbed the phone. Sure enough, Ruth had come through with the contact info for her web designer.

"Never mind. Gotta run. You'll be on tonight?"

"Of course. See you then."

Malachi took two minutes to run down and spring his

ship from the repair facility. At least that way when he did have time to play he'd be ready to go. With a final check that he'd set himself to be able to scoot out on a mission as soon as he logged back in, he exited the game and opened a web browser.

He liked the website for the Fairview, but there was nothing wrong with checking out other references just to be sure before making contact.

"You sure you won't come to church with us?" Ruth frowned as she signed.

He shook his head. Sunday morning was hard enough with everyone staring at Ruth signing during the sermon and special music. And then, out in the foyer, anyone who tried to talk to him either yelled, as if that was somehow going to help, or spoke slowly as if it was his brain that had been injured and not his ears. Both made it more challenging to read lips. He didn't need that on Wednesday night, too. "You don't have to babysit me. I'm okay."

"Don't you think if you were around them more it would help? The people at church are really nice, Mal."

"I believe you. I'm just...it's hard to be the weird new kid again. I thought that was behind me. In D.C., even if the people didn't know a deaf person personally they'd been exposed to enough differences that they could just treat me like a person without any adjective attached. I don't want to be 'the deaf guy.'" Mal threw his hands in the air when he finished signing and turned to head upstairs to the room he shared with his brothers at the B&B. And that was another thing they needed to address. Sharing a room with them temporarily was fine. But now that they were all settling here? Something had to give. And Ruth needed the space back, anyway. He'd seen her telling people she was booked up when, in reality, it was just her brothers taking up space.

Ruth touched his arm.

He turned, flinching inside at the sorrow written on her face.

"I'm sorry. You didn't have to move out here. If it's that bad...you don't have to stay." Her shoulders fell.

Was it possible to be a bigger jerk? He held out his arms and waited for her to walk into them. Since it was just Ruth, he could speak without worrying she was listening for the telltale signs of his deafness. "I'm glad to be here. If you're all here, then it's where I need to be. It's just...hard. And...I miss Mom and Dad."

Ruth leaned back and held his gaze, her eyes filling with tears. "I do too. Every day. I thought the years were supposed to make it easier."

He smiled and kissed her forehead before releasing her and tucking his hands in his pockets. With Ruth it was never an issue to talk without signing. Even if he didn't know what he sounded like. Half the time he imagined it was still the voice he remembered from his childhood, but it had to have changed as he'd grown up. Maybe, if he was lucky, he sounded a little bit like Dad. At least in his mind, Dad's baritone had been warm. Friendly. "Do you need me to go tonight?"

"No. No, I don't need you there for me. I just think you might find something there for you."

He scoffed but didn't ask exactly what she had in mind. As a recently engaged woman, Ruth was probably scouting the single ladies with an eye toward her brothers. But he'd been in high school when he'd given up on the delusion that he'd ever marry. The few deaf girls he'd dated had wanted him to turn his back on his hearing friends. And the hearing girls had treated him like he was a project. No. He was better off imagining love with someone like Scarlet Fire online than trying to navigate the real thing.

Malachi clicked on the mission, double checked that he had all the required equipment on board, and opened the map. He chose the first star system he'd need to visit and set the ship in motion. It wasn't instantaneous transport, which made the game a little more fun. Things could go wrong en route. There were pirates for one, and the handful of people who were irked at him for beating them to prizes. Most of them got over it and remembered it was just a game. But there were others who needed a stiff dose of reality. He tried to steer clear.

"Started without me?" Scarlet Fire's chat message popped up.

"Just barely. You can still join if you want."

"Sound good. I'll beam in?"

"Perfect." Malachi closed out of the armor customizing screen he'd been in and ran through the halls of his ship to the transportation hub. He verified that it was her and clicked to allow her to join the party. Her avatar materialized. He swallowed. It wasn't as if he didn't run into roughly the same avatar all the time—you could only customize your clothes and hair—but something about hers always made his heart stop. Which probably meant he needed to get a real life. "Welcome. We'll hit the first system in about two minutes. How was your day?"

"Got a new client. Always a good day. Even better, they're a referral from a previous client and they're local."

"Don't you do web design? Why does local matter?"

"Doesn't necessarily. But sometimes it helps if there are hiccups." Her avatar's hair color changed from bright red to blonde. "What do you think?"

"It's different."

"Is that good or bad? Was trying to go a little more real to life." The hair changed back. "Maybe that's not a good thing?"

She was a blonde. It didn't fit his mental image. Not surprising as he'd essentially un-animated her avatar and dressed her in normal clothes when he was forming it. But...blonde worked, too. "No, I liked it. It just took me by surprise."

"Don't you ever want people to know the real you?"

He shook his head and tapped the keys to dock the star ship at the port where they'd find the first leg of their mission. The best part of online multi-player games was having the chance to be who he really was without first waiting for people to get over the fact that he was deaf. "Not really."

Scripture quoted by permission. Quotations designated (NIV) are from THE HOLY BIBLE: NEW INTERNATIONAL VERSION®. NIV®. Copyright © 1973, 1978, 1984 by Biblica. All rights reserved worldwide.

Cover design ©Book Cover Bakery.

Cover art photos ©iStockphoto.com/heather_mcgrath, ©retrostar used by permission.

Published in the United States of America by Elizabeth Maddrey

www.ElizabethMaddrey.com

SUMMER'S GLORY

www.ingramcontent.com/pod-product-compliance
Lightning Source LLC
Chambersburg PA
CBHW020441270626
47155CB00022B/798